Betrayal, passion, adventure, primal sex, and a fight to the death.

Mating a 26th century Oracan Bounty Hunter with a 18th century pirate has its little glitches.

Bounty hunter Talos bows to pressure to bring his mate home for the completion of his strict warrior culture's bonding ritual. Aidan, displaced 18th century Earth pirate— light-fingered, sly, charming and understandably naive about the new world he's been thrust into— can't wait. Even if it turns out someone wants him dead. The 26th century looks different, but it turns out to be a lot like his old life!

Genetic Snare

#2 in the Details Series

Laura Baumbach

Published by
MLR Press, LLC
3052 Gaines Waterport Rd.
Albion, NY 14411

Visit ManLoveRomance Press, LLC on the Internet:
www.mlrpress.com

Cover Art by Spacepixel
Editing by Kris Jacen

Print format: ISBN# 978-1-934531-07-5
eBook format available

Issued 2017

Dedication

This book is dedicated to my editing staff, Kris Jacen, MLR Press's Editor in Chief, and Christie Nelson, both of whom made this book possible in so many ways. I appreciate their dedication, hard work and friendship. They make author's dreams into shared adventures for readers.

This is also dedicated to all my loyal readers. You have waited fourteen years for this.

I hope it gives you joy.

xoxox

Chapter One

There it was again, that eerie, exciting, almost sickening twist in his gut that made his bowels clench and his cock ache even before the rebellious shaft in his pants unfurled. It was unnatural to be so aroused by the mere thought of another person. Unnatural. Annoying. Frustrating. *Thrilling.*

But the beast's spell had been cast over him and there would be no breaking it as far as Aidan Maymon could see. Voodoo from a great hulking sea serpent, stronger than any he'd seen in all his twenty-some years as a pirate on the Caribbean. No charms or magic talismans, not even the ones his mother's Ceme religious beliefs had taught him as a lad before he went to sea as a cabin boy, could break it. In fact, the bewitching grew stronger every day.

Aidan could feel it growing heavier, yanking at his insides like he'd swallowed lead from the old blunderbuss that he had once kept tucked into the sash around his waist. Back before he'd been snatched from the ocean by the interfering beast that had pulled him from his own adventurous time and brought him to this confusing place called 'space' in a future so far ahead of him that even the people weren't all humans and the Earth was a dot in the night sky somewhere too far away for him to even see.

Granted his immediate future had been one of death by drowning or shark bite, courtesy of a mutinous mob, if his abductor hadn't shanghaied him when he did, but some days he wondered if that wouldn't have been better. Then there were no limits on his movements, his language, his games of sport or his tendency to acquire things by 'accident'. He had lived his life as a freeman and was to die that way.

Now he was a captive, both body and soul, to Talos, a delightful, horrible beast of a creature. A bounty hunter of all things! He was held hostage by ties he didn't understand, a life devoid of ocean, ship, captain's status, and personal freedoms. In their place he had been given a safe harbor, a healthy body unmarred by the disease of 18th century pirate life on Earth, and a lover that turned his insides to jellyfish with a mere thought.

Oh, and he was *alive*. Not that he would admit it to anyone else, but more alive than at any other time in his short life. Talos made him experience things he never thought possible before and the people and events on board this place were fascinating and intriguing to him. At was almost as if he was living a dream. Torture of the best kind. But he missed the trappings of his old life.

It still irritated him that Marius Webb, the Commander of the vessel they lived on—Pathos Six others called it—a sort of giant, anchored ship in the sky, refused to allow him to carry a pistol anymore.

Or a cutlass.

Or a knife.

Or a lock pick.

Or a...

Churning in his groin pushed at the bitter thought, desire overriding everything else.

Sexual escapades from his past had been nothing more than rough trade, hapless, hurried fumbles in a deserted hold or over a ship's railing. That was life aboard ship, whether pirate ship or Her Majesty's naval vessels. It had its pleasurable moments, but hadn't prepared Aidan for the type of coupling Talos demanded from him.

Nothing in his memory came close to the feelings and pleasure the massive bounty hunter had shown him. Talos of Menalon was a fierce warrior with a chiseled, attractive face. He was one of the largest of the Oracan Aidan had seen so far. His huge, heavy body was a mass of curves and lean dips with every muscle defined and highlighted by a natural sheen on his gray flesh. Each bulging, sinewy strip of flesh weaving around his limbs and torso led to another, forming an impressive tapestry of immense strength and power. His thick, protective skin had a soft gleam, its harsh gray color making charcoal shadows in the shallow dips of his body's contours.

Aidan was fascinated by the dull, gray ridges and nubs of bone on his chest that spread out in a regular pattern, dotting the valleys of his broad chest wall and breasts then tapering down to disappear near his groin. Their sharp, ragged edges belied their sensual nature and the part they played in Oracan biochemistry. Aidan's ravenous attraction with the hunter was the unique cock and other dangling bits the alien boasted, but Aidan suspected it all had more to do with the depth of feeling and attraction Talos had for him. He had never known a possessive lover or one that made him feel so many thrilling, terrifying things.

At times, he felt like he'd been crimped, pressed into service, but he knew that wasn't true. Kidnapped, yes, but Talos had saved his life at the same time. If the bounty hunter hadn't snatched him from the hands of his mutinous crew, Aidan would be now be sleeping in a watery Caribbean grave with Davy Jones.

And over seven hundred years would have passed.

Aidan hadn't aged during the time jump. His young, lean body gloried in arousal and craved satisfaction. A satisfaction that he suspected he could only get with a tussle in the berth of his lover. Talos had explained it was his body changing to adapt to Oracan mating, brought on by their exchange of fluids, but Aidan still suspected magic was at the heart of it.

He'd seen a man bewitched once, cursed by a spell from an exotic, lovely but vile priestess. Now he knew what that man must have felt like. Only weeks ago it'd taken Talos's physical presence before Aidan's body began to yearn for a bit of buggery. Now all that was required was a glance at the solid, towering, gray beast he bunked with and his knob was sword-fighting its way out of his trousers to do the deed. He was bewitched, no doubt about it.

Movement in the larger living area drew his attention. Talos had returned from gathering supplies he wanted for some celebration that was approaching. Aidan had stayed out of the way, preoccupied with his growing desire to be at Talos's side constantly.

Unnatural.

Unnecessary.

Unmanly.

And still, at this very moment, his spine tingled and his breathing became labored. An ache under his breast bone pulled his hand to his sternum to rub at his chest. In a flash, Aidan was off the bed and into the water closet, putting distance between them. At least for a little longer.

§ § § §

Aidan leaned his head back and let the hot water flow over his body, losing himself in the delicious decadence of the steamy, unnatural rain. The majority of things and people in his new lover's twenty-sixth century world were perplexing, but this hot, luxurious running water was amazingly pleasant. He found he almost enjoyed bathing.

But by far, his favorite part was the sex he and his powerful bounty hunter indulged in while in the shower. He had been introduced to his alien lover's unique and expert sexual skills in this very room along with the fine art of kissing another man and enjoying it.

He wasn't a virgin to man-on-man sex by any means, but the tender, rough, thrilling sex they shared was so much different with his brawny, stoic warrior than any Aidan had experienced with sailors during his seafaring days. Sex was now mindboggling, blissful. Aidan couldn't get enough of it.

Which was why he was presently wasting away his time taking too long in the indoor rain, hoping Talos would join him.

When his skin started to wrinkle, Aidan gave up and stepped out of the shower area, disappointed when the glorious waterfall instantly stopped. He liked the sound of it falling almost as much as the feel. It was the closest he'd gotten to being outside in nature for ages. The space station was interesting, but there was no wind against his face, no salt air to tease his nose, no sunshine to warm his skin, or thunder to rumble through his bones. Not even a tiny grain of gritty, warm sand to be found. He missed the feel of the ship's wheel under his hand. Life had definitely changed.

Ignoring the drying vents that had turned on the moment the water had stopped, Aidan shook himself all over like a dog coming out of the ocean surf, water flinging everywhere. He squeezed the moisture out of what little hair Dr. Rice had left of his once waist-length locks, resenting the doctor's diligent efforts all over again. After all, what had been the harm of a few dead bugs? They were dead, matted in his hair, yes, but *dead*. Scalping him like a barbarian head hunter had been extreme for the sake of that accursed cleanliness thing they all harped on and on about.

Shaking his head in silent, lingering resentment, he walked to the exit, but drew up short when the door stayed closed. Normally, the smooth wall knew he was coming and slid out of the way.

Almost afraid of the magical contraption, he touched his fingertips to the cool metal. When it didn't budge, he leaned closer, an ear tentatively pressed to the surface. Talos was on the other side of the door. He could sense him. He could hear the occasional, low growl the hunter usually made when he was doing something he found frustrating coming from the bedroom they shared. The sound made his cock jump, its full length reached in seconds. Aidan's entire body was flushed and tingling.

Earlier in the day, Commander Marius and Dr. Jaclyn Rice had insisted the two of them join them for a feast to celebrate the old custom of Christmas. A large group of humans on the space station had joined in on the festivities, playing games and exchanging tokens. None of which Aidan recognized and some he didn't understand.

In a jovial mood, Dr. Jaclyn had coaxed Aidan into promising to tell a group of the stations school children about how he had celebrated the Christmas holiday in the Caribbean. Aidan suspected she did it to gain a bit more of Talos's ire. Things were less tense between the hunter and the doc since their last adventure together, but there was no kinship among them as there was between Talos and Commander Marius.

He considered the merits of telling the truth about his usual drinking until he could barely stand, pickpocketing the crowds at the traditional Jonkonnu celebrations, and then spending said procured funds at the local whore house versus limiting himself to describing the colorful masked Cow and Head dancers, the massive feasts of pork and fruit, and the fun of the sweets and games. He made up his mind by giving them a little of both to make up for the good doctor having put her cutting blade to his prized hair.

With their friends and the majority of the human population on the space station caught up in the holiday, the fuss and ritual seemed to kindle a sort of frustrated restlessness in the big, stoic warrior.

Aidan didn't understand it. Oracans didn't celebrate the Earth holiday. And since, Aidan had been banned from picking pockets *on the station*—a fine point Aidan didn't intend to bring to anyone's notice—and drinking to excess, the holiday was really just another day. He would miss the music and the dancing, but gift-giving and religious expressions were best left to others.

He pushed aside thoughts of the celebration and concentrated on getting out of the water closet he was apparently locked in. Pounding an impatient fist, he hollered into the place where the door opened each time, oblivious to fact it was a sealed seam.

"You bloody beast! Are you fixing to let me come to bed with you, mate, or am I to make me berth in here for the night!"

He tossed his wet hair out of his eyes, smiling at the muffled growl that answered him from the bedroom. At least the domineering bastard didn't plan on leaving him here. Aidan was suddenly looking forward to the night.

The burly alien bounty hunter had capture his heart, as well as his body, when he had rescued him from the ocean depths while shanghaiing him. It had been the strangest and best thing that had ever happened to Aidan and he was living every fascinating day to the fullest, curses and bewitching to boot.

Being thrust seven hundred years into the future was confusing, but his mate had made it bearable and enticing. Having a male lover he could openly call his own and share his bed with was a new and exciting experience. It was the rest of the constraints this world put on him that were intolerable. He tugged self-consciously at the bounty band permanently encircling his wrist, chafing at the light metal that warmed against his skin.

His spirit needed freedom even if his heart and body were captive.

Suddenly, the door popped open. The room was awash in bright lights. He had no idea where they came from, the colors just *were*, peeking out from behind objects and edging furniture and walls. The sharp bite of cloves, ginger and cinnamon, all coveted spices to a seafaring man, made his nose wrinkle. Pale candlelight flickered around the room, columns of dancing white light perched on every surface that could support them safely. The effect was exotic, festive. It all brought a smile to his lips.

Shaking off the lingering water droplets, Aidan's cock bobbed, poking the warm air like a cutlass at the ready. Stepping out of the rain closet naked, his usual walk turned into a sexy saunter.

Talos stood in the center of the room, all seven feet, three hundred-plus-pounds of gray-skinned muscle, naked of his usual attire of multi-pocketed, thin pants and boots. His broad, heavily muscled chest and arms invited touching and exploration. Aidan's fingers twitched in anticipation.

He watched, intrigued as always, as Talos sniffed the air. The hunter's cock instantly swayed, growing longer, as if reaching out to Aidan.

Aidan pressed close, making Talos's skin drip with the lingering water beads on his body. Aidan rubbed his open palms over the hard cartilage nubs on the warrior's chest. He didn't understand why, but he knew the act inflamed the hunter's desires.

"You've redecorated a bit whilst I was enjoying the rain." He smiled up into Talos's brilliant violet eyes, a wry twist to his full lips. "Like the candlelight, but can't say the green and red lights do much for your eyes, luv." He tipped his chin in a questioning tilt. "What's the grand occasion?"

Grabbing onto Aidan's wet, slippery ass and tightly muscled thighs, Talos kneaded the smooth flesh, reluctant restraint in his expression. "Humans seem to want to be reminded of their birthplace during this religious ritual time." Talos lightly kissed Aidan's lips. "I wanted to give you pleasure."

"Know a better way for ye to give me pleasure, luv."

The pirate seized the opportunity and pulled Talos's hairless, thick-skinned head back down to ravage the hunter's mouth. Talos was the first male to actually kiss him like a true lover. Aidan had discovered he liked doing it. Besides, the alien tasted like brandy, Aidan's favorite beverage.

After one startled second, Talos returned the voracious attention, stroking Aidan's tongue with his own, drawing a low moan of pleasure from his lover.

Aidan's fully erect cock jabbed against Talos's thigh. The pirate squirmed trying to get closer then gave up and shoved Talos backward. Still entwined, they both bounced on the large bed behind them. Using the advantage of being able to crawl up the hunter's taller frame, Aidan refused to release his hold keeping their lips sealed together and his tongue down Talos's throat.

Straddling the hunter's chest, Aidan tucked his knees into both of the Oracan's underarms, planted his bare ass on Talos's sternum and sat up straight, his eager cock bobbing in the air between them.

"Never celebrated Christmas the way your commander and Dr. Jaclyn do." A quick glance around them took in all the special effort Talos had gone to. "This is all lovely, mate, but it doesn't mean much to me." He rubbed his palms over Talos's chest, delighted in the way his usually stoic lover seemed to melt into the bed.

A frown pinched together the nubbed ridges that ran above Talos's eyes. "With all the English sailors around Jamaica during your time period in Earth's history, I thought you'd have acquired their customs just like you did their speech patterns."

"Learned to speak the King's English on board ships, from the sailors in port, but me mum raised me. Despite me Spanish father's looks I got saddled with, she's a native of the islands, luv. 'Sides, the

Caribbean does things amight differently." Aidan caught a fleeting glance of disappoint as it skittered across his lover's face. "But it were a lovely and kind thought. Got any other lovely thoughts to share? If not..." He wiggled his ass, still resting on Talos's chest, and watched the light in the hunter's eyes turn heated and bright. "I have a few suggestions of me own."

Slowly sliding backward off the warrior's long, thick body, Aidan evaded Talos's grasping hands and got to his feet.

"Caribbeans celebrate Jonkonnu, that's Christmas to you, with dance. Tricksters parade down the streets and entice villagers to pay them for songs. If you pay you get a blessing on you and if you don't you get a wicked verse to embarrass you. But the dancing is the best part of the fun. I'll show you." Aidan shook his hair out of his eyes and ran his hands over his naked body in slow, provocative strokes. "Consider it me gift to you."

Grabbing a slim wooden candle holder, Aidan blew out the flame and removed the candle. "Listen to the beat." Taking a firm grip on the candle holder, he began beating out a primal one-two-three beat on the nearby table top. After a few minutes, he tossed the make-shift musical instrument in the air to Talos. The hunter caught in one beefy fist.

"Beat it like I just showed you. On the floor." He winked and gave Talos a cocky smile. "Easier if you can hear the music playing in me head, too, luv."

A deep, pulsing rhythm filled the room as Talos began beating the wooden holder on the floor, occasionally adding a tap to the side of the bed. It was a primitive ritual filled with sexual implications. Talos's gaze locked on Aidan's naked, now swaying body, as his fist beat out the tune. His free hand found his own thick cock and he stroked it in time to the movement of Aidan's hips.

Not having indulged much in dancing during his previous life, Aidan still had a smooth, flowing sway to his walk under the best of conditions. Years of ship board life had taught him that.

Aidan spread his legs, bent his knees and moved his arms through air, mimicking all the many dancers he had witnessed in his early years on the islands. The dancers had been exciting and athletic. He tried to copy some of their more suggestive and sensual moves, picking ones that accented his bare state and bobbing cock.

He stomped closer to Talos, his gaze taking in his lover's every reaction, watching for the moment when all the violet color disappeared from the hunter's eyes and only the yellow remained. By then he knew the warrior would be ravenous for him. There would be no comment or hesitation, just hard and powerful, satisfying.

Hips rotating and thrusting in time to the music, Aidan edged closer to the bed. The primal beat invaded his blood and his heart seemed to pulse along with it. A fine sheen of sweat covered him and he shivered, adding a shimmy to the dance. Talos gasped. Aidan did it again and grinned when Talos swallowed hard and continued to stare, the candlestick falling harder, moving faster.

The stoic hunter lay propped up, stretched out on the side of the bed silently watching, waiting, and beating out the tempo. When he was only two feet away from the bed, Aidan turned and presented his firm, smooth ass to his lover. Reaching around to spread his cheeks open, Aidan found his arms pinned to his side and his body lifted off the floor, then deposited on the bed. Talos rubbed his face over Aidan's skin, inhaling deeply. The pulsing beat was only an echo in the room.

Talos made a rich, deep clicking 'ta-ti' sound at the back of his throat and gave his young lover a look Aidan thought of as poker-hot, lustful need. Aidan scrambled over Talos's body and positioned his ass against Talos's groin. He stroked his open palms over his lover's breast plates.

The pirate's ass clenched and his asshole spasmed, anxious to be filled. A blunt poke from behind fanned his needs higher. He scooted back until his ass rested directly above Talos's impatient cock. Talos's strong hands aided his movements.

Aidan hissed, and then panted as the suction cup-tipped tubulars surrounding the Oracan's long, stout cock tapped the sensitive flesh of his spread hole. Each tip grabbed and nipped at his body until it found a suitable spot to latch onto at the tender opening.

The sensation was of needle-like jabs and soft, teasing sucks that felt like tiny, nipping kisses to his skin. As usual, several questing tubes burrowed out, seeking the delicate flesh of his scrotum and the bulging root of his shaft where it attached to the floor of his perineum.

Moaning, Aidan rolled his head on his shoulders. He raised up as far as the attached tubulars would allow him, swiftly reached behind, and guided Talos's eager cock to his opening. With a half-lidded glance at Talos to be sure the warrior was watching, he slowly sank down onto the long, smooth shaft, gasping and grunting as it slid into him, the cock's own alien ability to slither and undulate into his body making him shudder with indescribable pleasure.

Grinding his ass, the opening to his body fluttered and clenched around Talos's cock as the growing shaft thickened and moved inside of him. His own cock bobbed between his wide-spread thighs, leaking pearls of milky white. His swollen, hot nipples ached to be touched. His stomach rolled and clenched, his mind hazy with the white-hot flush of sexual hunger.

Steadying himself with one hand on his lover's pressure sensitive, heaving chest, Aidan began to raise and lower his hips, savoring the delicious rippling effect that the combination of his movement and Talos's cock's wiggling produced. A warm, tight fist engulfed his cock and began a slow, leisurely caress up and down the length in time to Aidan's rhythmic hips movements.

The hunter shifted and Aidan fell forward. He grabbed the hunter's face for a kiss, gasping as the change in position shifted the shaft inside of him to rub directly over his prostate. He shuddered at the shot of sizzling sparks that shot up his spine from deep inside his gut. He pulled Talos's face to him and rubbed his own wet, hot lips over the hunter's willing mouth.

When they finally broke off the embrace, Aidan panted as if he had just climbed to the top of his ship's crow's nest and back down again.

"Could get to like celebrating the holidays with you, luv. Maybe we need a few Christmas traditions of our own, eh?" Aidan hissed and wiggled his ass against Talos's clutching, sucking groin.

Talos wove a hand through Aidan's hair and turned the pirate's face so he could purr in his ear, proclaiming, "We'll have decades together to make them. Christmas dance will be the first one." He gave his 'I love you' clicking sound of 'ta-ti' and another deep, blistering kiss.

Talos shifted his hips, plunged his cock deeper and rolled them both over on the bed. Latched together by their groins and mouths, Aidan had no choice but to ride out the action.

Once Talos had Aidan under him, the hunter began thrusting into Aidan's ass in long, hard, deep strokes that brushed over his prostate both coming and going. White lights exploded in Aidan's head and his limbs felt like they were on fire.

The hunter's snake-like cock wriggled and squirmed inside of him, touching places no one else ever had, no one ever could. It sent shivers of exotic bliss up his spine. The sucking kisses from the attached tiny tubulars heightened his awareness of the tender flesh around his hole. He reveled in the burn and stretch of the tight muscles that guarded his opening.

Every stroke out was like a rough caress. Every forceful thrust in jarred his pleasure core and sent bursts of flame through his entire body. His flesh gleamed in the candlelight, sweat glistening on his arms and belly.

Without warning, Aidan's climax barreled down on him. He arched and cried out, a startled bellow of cosmic release. The orgasm peaked with a staggering force. Aidan floated on the crest of it for an incredibly long time, the momentum sustained by Talos's continuing thrusts to his prostate and the sucking actions of the tubulars, some of which and burrowed inside his ass along with Talos's shaft and were now nipping and sucking at the nerve filled ring of muscle from the hyper-sensitive inside.

A wave of wetness washed into his channel. Talos was preparing to climax. He squeezed his ass tight and clamped down on his lover's shaft, making the now rapid-fire thrusts more powerful. Talos growled deep in his throat, a throaty, animal sound, the vibrations echoing through Aidan's chest.

Talos's guttural reaction shot a thrill through the pirate. He loved being able to affect the stoic warrior like this, loved knowing he could take the hunter down to his most primitive level. He liked knowing Talos was just as hungry for him as he was for the warrior. It lessened his fears.

A sudden gush of wet heat flooded his gut. Aidan gasped and squirmed harder, the thick liquid of Talos's fluids coating his insides, his body absorbing it. The alien cum invaded every corner of his body, making him a part of Talos, altering his body and binding the two of them together. Some days he resented it, but not at this moment.

Aidan glanced at the flickering candles, and the muted red and green lights still burning softly in the room. Talos was right. Humans did want to be reminded of their home at the holidays. Unnatural as it was, bewitched or cursed, he was home. Here in his beast of a sea serpent's embrace.

Talos eased down, took Aidan into his arms and rolled them over. Aidan balanced on Talos's chest, then slowly sat up, the squirming alien cock still buried deep inside of him, its length slender and long when he needed it to be to accomplish movement. It grew thick and firm, shortening and less active once he was comfortably upright. He felt plugged like a cork in a jug of rum, his hole stretched wide, a pleasant burn making him arch his back to intensify the sensation, the hunger rising again, need for more building at the base of his spent but firm cock. He raised his hips until the cock inside him grew thicker in protest and the tubulars sucked harder, both pulling him back down. He obliged with a forceful thrust of his own and then pulled up again.

"More, runt?" The burning, yellow glint in the hunter's eyes almost made Aidan come again. Talos was rising to the challenge. Aidan leaned his weight on his hands, spreading his palms over the cartilage ridges on the Oracan's chest. He wet a thumb with his tongue then painted a chest nub with the slick spit. He could feel the rumble of passion rolling under his hands in Talos's chest.

"You've been boarded, me hearty." With a wicked smile, Aidan clenched his ass and rocked back and forth, defeating the tubulars' effort to slow him down. He could feel that growing, odd sensation swirling through his body, almost as if his blood was boiling like thundering ocean waves, and reason was swept away with the tide. Lust ruled his every thought, and all of them were of Talos. "Surrender, luv, or use your sword."

"I think I'd better disarm you first." Suddenly Aidan was pulled forward, the tubulars instantly disengaged. Talos's cock slithered out and was gone. He barely had time to cry out at the loss when his stiffened cock was swallowed whole. The battle had begun.

Chapter Two

The candles had stuttered out leaving the room draped in pale gray shadow. It was a comfortable darkness, one Talos found restful, a spectrum of low light in which his keen eyesight functioned well. Being able to see in the dark, and underwater, was a definite advantage for stalking prey. Talos was monetarily sated and fully rested after a few hours of sleep. The genetic mandate to claim his new mate at an increasingly awkward rate hadn't affected his hunter's sense of alertness and physical stamina. His body was created for the claiming ritual of his race, unlike his unprepared human lover. They would have to bring this need to an end soon if Aidan was to survive it.

Aidan had passed out immediately after his last climax. Talos had waited until he was sure his spent fluids had been absorbed by Aidan's system, then he had gently lifted the slight human off his body and deposited the limp pirate on the bed beside him.

The sight of his lover flushed with the lingering heat of their coupling, limbs akimbo, Aidan's beautiful face looking even younger with sleep, stirred his need to take the man one more time. But the instinct to provide and protect his new fragile mate was even more overwhelming than his nearly constant urge to mate.

He started to reach for the thin sheet lying in a tangled heap at the foot of the bed to cover Aidan and thus lessen temptation. Instead, he rose up and walked out of the room. Aidan preferred to sleep uncovered, just as he did. Less encumbrances to a quick awakening and a fast draw of a waiting weapon. A warrior's way, one of the many ways the two of them were alike. Despite the centuries and culture differences between them, they were made from a similar mold.

A soft, insistent chime drew him to the side console in the main living area. Ignoring his unclothed state, Talos acknowledged the signal and opened the outside communication channel. The regal image of his elder brother Zeban appeared, but the robes of High Principle he usually wore were absent. A personal call. Talos instantly became cautious.

Fist over his left abdomen, Talos moved his hand up and over his heart in the traditional greeting of their people. "Honor and compassion, Zeban."

Zeban returned the greeting. Talos caught the glint of amusement in his brother's expression as the elder Oracan glanced at Talos's full naked image. "Am I interrupting something, my brother?"

"Nothing of interest to a High Principle."

"Ah, but I'm not speaking as a Council member right now, little brother. I'm asking as a concerned family member."

"Concerned about what?"

"Aidan's health. How is your little human?"

"He's jake. Don't get in a twist over him."

"I assume in your beloved ancient Earth gangster slang that means you think he's fine. It would be pleasurable to see him again. He is...entertaining."

"He's getting used to the space station. Let him catch up on seven hundred years of his own culture before he tackles a new world, Zeban."

"He seemed highly adaptable to me. It's not everyone who can take on an entire troop of thugs, save the fair Dr. Rice from death, defeat a fellow like Barlow in hand-to-hand combat and still manage to blow up an island in the process of winning the battle."

"It was only half an island and that was an accident. And he got the drop on Barlow in a sword fight. What idiot in his right mind challenges a pirate who grew up with a blade in his hand to a sword fight and expects to win?"

"It is fortunate we erased those events in his future, is it not?"

"Yeah, sure."

"You don't sound...sure."

"I'm sure." He sounded sure, but the tiny squint at the corner of his brother's one eye didn't fit. Zeban had always been able to read his mood since they were children. His older brother had the people skills, while he was given the physical talents. "Only Oracans can time sense, you know that." Talos straightened his spine, donning the mantle of strength and confidence a hunter was renowned for possessing.

"He's safe and well." The vision of Aidan, exhausted and spent after another marathon bout of lovemaking flashed through his mind, his lover's tanned skin flushed and slick with sweat while the bonding fever glinted bright in his dark eyes. Guilt rose up like bile and burned Talos's throat. "And if he isn't, I'll take care of him."

"Do you think he may not be safe? Have there been new enemies stalking him?"

"Not since Barlow. Why?"

"There have been a series of...incidences here."

"What kind of incidences? Involving who?"

"Menalon. An accident in the marketplace. One that, at closer inspection, seems less accidental than was first thought."

Old pain and resentment boiled up, but Talos wouldn't deny his deep-seated family bond. "Was our father injured?"

"No." Zeban was quick to answer, but Talos felt he was holding back. "The event did put a strain on him. He *is* approaching his edge year."

The rites of passage to the land beyond was a complex celebration of honor Talos had little time for. "What else happened?"

"Yesterday there was a fire."

"Where?"

"My personal lodgings. No one was hurt beyond Penna suffering a few minor burns trying to douse the flames. But this morning, an automated short distance freighter exploded as it jumped the time division. A freighter that had just completed a total inspection."

"Let me guess. The freighter was one belonging to the cashe."

"Yes, it was Menalon's newest."

"What's the wire on the attacks?"

"Information? Very little. Whoever it is, they've covering their tracks well, I'm afraid. I was hoping you would agree to return to Oracan and help. You are the trained hunter, Oracan's most celebrated Hunter. Surely, you can set aside old wounds for this? There are others besides Menalon endangered by the attacks."

Honor and compassion were more than just words of greeting to Talos. He lived them every minute of his existence, had built his life upholding the essence of the code and honoring the details of the hunt. He could distance himself from his father and the family politics by living with humans on Pathos Six, but he couldn't turn his back on his brother.

"Fine. I'll need a little time to make some arrangements."

"For your pirate?" Zeban's tone changed just enough to make Talos pause. Something was up.

"Yes."

"Bring him. I doubt he wants to be separated from you at this point. The entire cashe is anxious to meet your little human mate."

"He's not coming."

"You have to bring him some—"

"No, I don't." Aidan wasn't an Oracan. He didn't have to endure the rituals other mating couples did. He had enough to deal with adjusting to his new life. Surely, Zeban understood this. "If it's as dangerous there as you say it is, he'll be safer on Pathos."

"If I know your pirate, he'll have something to say about that."

"I'll have Marius put a leash and muzzle on him and stash him under lock and key. Aidan stays here."

"Rites of—"

"He stays here." He gave his brother the look that had been known to stop cold-blooded killers in their footsteps. Silence fell, the air heavy. Talos let the moment go on a few seconds more. "I'll make contact when I leave Pathos."

The scent in the room changed subtly moments ago and now Talos couldn't hold back his reaction. No other muscle in his body so much as twitched but Talos's cock responded, growing stout and dark with anticipation. Zeban couldn't help but notice and a smile tugged at his face, mirroring the one he wore at the start of their conversation.

"Take the time to dress, little brother. You'll need something more permanent to hang your weapons from. Of course, if you bring your pirate along, it just might work out for you."

"Funny man." Foregoing the formal salutation, Talos cut the transmission off before Zeban could wedge another word in. He stared at the blank monitor for moment. His mind raced at the prospect of returning to his planet again so soon, even if it was to in response to a summons for help. It was the last place he wanted to be, especially without Aidan.

Aidan. He inhaled a slow tantalizing breath, savoring the scent of his mate, tasting the sweat of Aidan's skin and the slight bitterness of his cum. The recent memory would have to do for now.

"Leash an' muzzle, luv?" The words had that blurry lilt to them that lack of education and a lifetime of slurring his words for effect had given the pirate's voice. As deceptive and endearing as the deviously sharp man the voice belonged to.

Talos turned to face his lover, disappointed the pirate had dressed before coming to him. But it was probably just as well, considering the hard look in Aidan's eyes.

"You plan on locking me in the brig or the hold with the rest of the animals?"

There was a glint of color in the pirate's collar length dark hair. The rattle of beads clicked seductively as Aidan titled his head. This was a new addition to the pirate's attire. Dr. Rice had removed all of Aidan's hair…embellishments when she had chopped off his hair to rid him of the lice and other dead creatures in it when Talos took him as bounty. Now the old beads were strung on a new cord and wrapped around a lock of silky, brown hair. "You got your beads back. I like them."

"Holiday gift from Dr. Jaclyn." Aidan nodded, making them rattle a bit. "Added one of her own, a magical one. Sticks to me sword if it gets near." He sounded distracted, talking gifts and beads with his mouth, but his unwavering dark stare spoke of other things to Talos, not all of them good.

"It has magnetic properties. Like in your old compass. It's drawn to some ancient metals like the forging your finer weapons are made from."

"Which is it? The ship's hold or the brig this time?"

"For the ninth time, this is a space station not a space ship. There is no hold." A narrowing of eyes was Aidan's only comment. "I was going to ask Marius and the doc to keep you company."

Aidan refused to glance at his beckoning cock. That was unusual. Aidan never failed to be lured into sexual play when they were alone. Most often, the pirate was the one who started it. Maybe he was unwell. Talos stepped closer and Aidan moved past him toward the door, taking effort not to touch as they passed each other. "I won't be gone long."

"Didn't sound simple." Aidan turned so he was only partially facing Talos, his gaze wandering the room, anywhere but on Talos.

"I can't refuse my brother's request to help."

"Then why refuse his request to bring me along?"

"That's different. There have been attacks on the family. I don't want to put you in danger."

"Think I can't look out for me self, luv?"

"You know better than that."

"Then it's settled. What should I take? Just me sword and a blade or two?"

"No, you're not going."

"Am."

"*Not.*"

"Ah, I see. So it was all pretty words an' speeches, then."

"What?"

"It's not changed. Ye can't be showing me off to your brethren. A man instead of a woman for your bunkmate."

"You're off your rocker. No one on Oracan objects to any choice in life mates."

"Then it's because I be pirate."

"*Was* a pirate. And no, that's not it."

"Not much left to object to, luv."

"Yes, there is. The bonding is affecting you faster than it does Oracans. Faster and harder. I can see it in your eyes, feel your body tremble with need from here. I can smell your sex, taste your cock's fluid in the air even now." Aidan backed away putting more space between them. Talos didn't follow. "I know you're trying to keep distance between us so you can stay in control, not give into the urges that are burning your insides to ash. I thought it would help if I wasn't here for a while. Let the fever burn out. Give you a chance to rest."

"'Tis that easy to be rid of me?"

"What? No!"

"Then why so eager to leave me behind?"

"I'm not."

"The last time you went there and left me here something unnatural happened."

"It wasn't unnatural."

"'Tis part of the curse."

"You aren't cursed. I told you it's a physical change from mating.

It's a natural process."

"For your people, luv. Not the likes of me. For me it be part curse. I be a marked man from the day we first crossed swords. I can feel it! Sometimes it be like a ghost walked right through me. All cold, gray and wet like ocean mist. Turns me guts to knots, it does." He ground his fist into his stomach as if that could untie the knots lodged deep inside. "Sometimes with bloody fear, sometimes with a raging want so big it barely lets me breath air."

"Time apart might help—"

"Belay that scurvy talk." Aidan made a slashing cut between them with his hand. His voice bounced off the walls and ceiling, pain and anger evident in the harsh tone. "You *are* me air, you great, *dense,* gray monster!" Then his voice lowered, sure and defiant, raging with passion and fury. "That's the part 'tis so frightening."

Without a glance back, Aidan burst out into the corridor, striding away as if Neptune himself was on his heels, nearly knocking over a startlingly pale human loitering in the hallway.

Talos was left to stare at an empty room.

Chapter Three

"Lost something, mate?"

In a busy part of the ship, Aidan paused near the magical small room that took him from one place and delivered him to new part of the ship without him having walked a step. It was disturbing. He preferred the many ladders and walkways tucked into the corners of the great ship, but he was in a hurry to put space between himself and the daft rock of a creature he lived with. In a hurry, but not so much of one that he didn't notice when he had a new shadow.

"You be traveling the same course since leaving me berth. What interest have ye in me?"

"I've been looking for an opportunity to meet you." The human stuck out his hand.

Aidan ignored it. He wasn't about to give over his sword hand to a stranger, whether there was a sword on his belt or not.

"Name's Opius Worth. I dabble in games of chance and skill. I heard you were a man who liked a bit of a wager." Worth fingered a coin-shaped bauble in his hand as he talked, an exaggerated gesture of rubbing his thumb over the ridged surface again and again.

"Always been a wagering man." Aidan grinned, but he could tell the coin wasn't gold or silver by the way the light failed to gleam properly off the surface. "But I gamble for real treasure, not bits of useless pot metal from foreign lands."

Anything not from his beloved Earth held little interest for him. The same went for the man. This human had an air about him that set Aidan's teeth on edge. He knew this type—con man, grifter, a biter. He didn't have time to beat him at his own game. Not now, anyway.

"Not got time to spend on a biter, mate. Maybe another time." Aidan set off at a fast jog, sliding past others in the hall with sure walk of a man navigating rough waters. He flew up an access ladder like a crow headed for the bird's nest.

§ § § §

"What?" Worth was thrown off by Aidan's foreign words and the direct approach, giving the pirate time to get lost in the milling passengers in the popular passageway. He called after Aidan, "What the nova is a biter?"

A new presence nudged Worth's elbow. "What happened?"

Worth turned to glance at the man. "He's not interested unless there is gold or silver on the table, Snow."

"So tell him there is. It's not like he's going to win anyway." Snow chuckled low and deep in his throat. "He'll actually *be* the prize. Where did he go? To the arboretum again?"

"Probably. It's the only place he goes alone from what I've seen over the last few days."

"Stop trying to con him and just grab him there. That plant park sinks of sulfur and 'M'. Not many humans spend time there."

"It's situated too near a security post." Worth frowned, but he tried to keep his expression casual for any curious by-passers.

"You're making this too hard. So we grab him someplace else. "

"Not if we can't separate him from that hunter for more than five decaseconds." Worth hissed, "You want to take an Oracan bounty hunter on?"

Snow sneered, but said nothing. He liked his heart intact in his chest and still beating, just like Worth did.

The two men moved to a shadowed corner by a busy entertainment stall, one of the many businesses in this part of the ship. "Maymon's a slippery one. It's taken me four days to get this close. The arboretum is our best chance of simply taking him if we can't convince him to come with us on his own."

"You're sure the buyer needs him alive?" Snow clenched his fists and cracked his knuckles, aching for action.

"Alive, yes." A new light came into Worth's hooded eyes. "One hundred percent healthy? Not necessarily. I've been reading up on that arboretum's contents. I have an idea." Worth slipped down the passage in the same direction Aidan had gone. Snow trailed behind him, interest clear in his predatory expression.

§ § § §

"You have that look on your face. Again."

"What look?" Talos knew it was a vain attempt to have the space station commander see his presence as anything more than a casual visit of a friend, but he did it anyway. One of the joys of having Marius Webb as his closest friend was the chance to indulge in bouts of uncensored banter.

Marius and he shared an interest in Earth history. The commander knew Talos had taught himself English by watching old salvaged Earth entertainment films from the early days of the invention of television. His favorite had been 1940's gangster movies and his conversations reflected the era's slang. It was sharp, bold and abrupt. It fit Talos to a tee.

"The look that says my life just got more complicated than it was before you breezed in here and plowed through my staff."

"I don't 'plow' through things. Humans just don't move very fast. Low self-preservation instincts."

Life as a solitary bounty hunter offered few opportunities to let down his guard. Especially when he needed an outlet to discuss the only other person beside Marius who accepted him completely as he was, killer instincts and all. Marius also had the dubious distinction of being one of only two humans who knew the real origin of the Oracan time travel technology, knowledge forbidden to outsiders.

"I know. It's amazing we've managed to survive this long as a race." That droll sense of humor eased a little of Talos's hesitancy.

Marius stood up from his desk and walked over to the open archway behind the hunter. Talos turned with him and they both watched Marius's new office assistant pour water over his hand, shrug calmly at Marius's questioning glance and then exit the antechamber at a brisk pace. "And you're right. My staff should have learned by now to duck and run the moment they see you."

"Exactly. It would save them from having to go see that dizzy dame of yours and save me from having to have this conversation with you."

"You know how much Dr. Rice likes seeing minor skin burns show up in her sickbay every time someone on this station 'bumps' into you." Marius eyed Talos's thick gray hide. "I know how much I like hearing about it afterward."

"Like I said, humans are too slow." Was it his fault humans were so frail their thin, sensitive skin burned when it came in contact with an Oracan? That is, every human but a certain pirate from seven centuries ago. "If you'd stop seeing that dame, your life would be a lot quieter, too."

Marius didn't respond, just sat, staring at him until Talos felt the man's attention start to shift from interested and mildly amused to exasperated. It didn't take humans long to make that jump.

"Well? Let me have it. What has Aidan done now? Where is he?" Such an impatient and impulse a race.

"Nothing." It was true. Aidan hadn't done anything to warrant the commander's attention, but he was the reason Talos was here. At least part of it. He closed his eyes and concentrated for a brief flash of time. "He's in the arboretum. His favorite place to avoid everyone. The air is putrid there, but it reminds him of life onboard ship."

Marius didn't look as if he even tried to hold back the smirk twisting his face into a grin. "Well, it's early yet. Let's give him time. I'm sure mischief will find him soon enough." Marius reached up and tapped Talos on the chest, knuckles striking the leather sash slung across the broad mounds of gray flesh and muscle. At six foot seven, Marius's height put him exactly one foot shorter than Talos's towering frame.

Turning away, Talos dropped into the large chair to the right of the desk. It automatically changed shape to accommodate his size and body build. "Everyone's a joker today."

He didn't bother to sound too affronted. The two of them had spent half their time these past few weeks dealing with the fallout from the pirate's attempts to adjust to every part of his new existence.

"Admit it, my friend." Marius took his seat behind his desk again. "You took the pirate away from his cut throat existence, but you haven't yet got a clue how to change a lifetime of, let's say, his less than savory social talents."

"Come on, what would a pirate be if he wasn't a *little* bit larcenous and conniving?"

"A law-abiding citizen on this space station."

"Then no one would need you or your storm troopers. Think of Aidan as job security."

"Security *personnel*. The Corporation does not employ storm troopers. And you're just upset because those are some of Aidan's better qualities."

"You *like* it when he nicks things from the other station dwellers?"

"No, I don't like it when he picks pockets! But it's easier to deal with than when he triggers security alarms, disables force fields and short circuits half the electronics on the station with a fork and a peach pit."

"The fork thing was a onetime jimmy."

"So far." Despite the chaos Aidan created, Marius truly did appear to like him. "Admit, it. Aidan Maymon, *your* life mate, is indisputably incorrigible. You're lucky most of the station likes him, me included. And you're even luckier that Jaclyn adores him. He's the only thing that keeps her from registering you as a hazard to human life and getting you banned from the station."

Marius tapped a control on his side table unit. Two short, square, transparent glasses appeared half full of a brownish liquid. He handed one to Talos and palmed the other himself. Both took a sip of the very old liquor and companionable silence settled over them. Ever the practical man, Marius brought the conversation back to his original question.

"Who else is prodding your not-so-funny bone today if it's not your pirate?"

Talos savored the bite of the smoky drink. It burned his throat, a pleasant rush of fire that warmed his skin. Whiskey may have been the drink of gangsters and molls but Talos preferred the smoother taste of brandy. Fine aged brandy from Earth, like this one. "Zeban."

"A message from the Oracan Council?"

There was enough controlled concern in Marius's tone that Talos added, "A personal call."

"What's happened?" Marius instantly transformed from friend to Commander of Pathos Six, guardian of the outer ring of this galaxy, protector of both The Corporation's interests and the life forms that called P6 home. "A High Principle wouldn't contact you directly unless there was something of major concern."

"Relax. You forget he's my brother. It was a personal call."

"Personal?" Marius's tone was interested, but casual. The man never pried. Having recently learned more about Oracans then he had ever wanted to, the commander knew the prudence of remaining ignorant of some things regarding the fierce warrior race. All the same, Talos knew the door was ajar if he wanted to talk. Marius would listen.

"He wants me to visit the cashe."

"That doesn't sound too ominous to me."

"Until you hear there have been attacks on my father's household, including sabotage one of Menalon's freighters. Zeban is concerned, they are all connected. The ones responsible haven't been rousted yet. He wants me to help."

"So you're going home?"

"I agreed to travel to Oracan to assist them in finding the sour apple. Home is here."

"Home is here because Aidan is here, yes?"

"And that's where I want to leave him. Here, where he's out of harm's way. Will you watch him?"

"No deal. The last time you left him behind, someone kidnapped him." Marius shook his head. "Seems theft is a natural part of him in so many ways."

"Look, Marius, I can't take him there. Not yet. If I do, the ritual laws will be enforced and he'll have to face the mating challenges. As a newly mated pair, decreed by the Council, family honor and political posturing will demand it."

"I'd ask if that as such a bad thing, but I still remember what Oracans consider to be 'relocation'."

"The mating ritual is brutal. Every couple who wishes to mate must survive the ritual challenges to prove they are fit to breed. Not everyone does."

"Oracan is a fierce warrior race. I know you are fierce, aggressive warriors by nature, but you aren't known for having easily ignited tempers. That's why they became peacekeepers throughout much of the galaxy. Surely the Council would recognize that the ritual wasn't designed for a human to complete. And you won't be breeding. They have to have an exception clause. What other outside races have had to do it?"

"None."

"None?"

"No other race has ever mated with an Oracan before. Our lines are pure."

"That's a problem. Galactic scale problem." Marius set his drink aside. "Lord, even when he hasn't done anything willfully wrong Aidan is the center of controversy." He drew a deep, thoughtful breath. "They'll accept him if he survives?"

"Yes. There are no exceptions for that, either. The Council won't be concerned about that. The chance the runt will survive is dodgy." Talos tossed back the brandy like it was water. "I limit my time on Oracan to Calls to Hunt so ritual, ancient laws, tradition and the whole damn Council stays out of my life."

"It's been hard since your brother's death."

"The Council is responsible for my brother's death, and my mother's death." His massive fist smashed the brandy glass down onto the desk, cracking the heavy glass. "And now they want to take Aidan from me."

"That's a bit harsh, Talos. Your brother was young, inexperienced. It was an unfortunate, but you can't really think anyone plotted his death, the Council or anyone else. You said yourself your mother honored the old ways by ending her life once she became terminally ill."

"My father did not have to agree."

"You know he did. It would have been disrespectful to her if he hadn't. She died with grace and honor, with her family at her side, like the great warrior and matriarch she was."

A chill rippled through his chest. "I'll never forget the way I felt when he slipped a shiv into her chest." The memory was as fresh as the day it had happened. So was the pain. "I can't forgive any culture that demands a dying warrior's early death."

"You're concerned Oracan traditions will hurt someone you care for."

"For a third time? Yeah, maybe. I can't control it, Marius. We're both deep in the snare." His voice was a deep growl, rumbling in his throat like restrained thunder. "Tradition is in our DNA. It's not just teachings, rituals, ideals, handed down. It's biological. Inescapable."

"Remember that when you think about Menalon and your mother's situation." Marius shook his head, gaze earnest and open. "Zeban wouldn't play into the Council's hands. He must have a plan of action if he wants you to bring Aidan."

"Zeban wants to make a show of family solidarity over my bonding with a human. Political enemies of my family are using it to try to weaken our placement in the governing house. Our family is one of the strongest caches on the planet. Bottom line, both sides are stacking the deck against us."

"Is it that bad? If your family is supporting you in such an open manner, isn't that a good thing?"

"The mating ritual lasts days. It's brutal for Oracans. How's the runt going to cheat the devil?"

"Aidan will surprise you. He always does me." Marius grinned and tipped his glass toward Talos in a silent, brotherly salute.

Just then amber lights began flashing and multiple alarms blared identifying the problem area. There was a fire on board.

"Runt!"

Marius shot from his seat. Talos still beat him out the door.

Chapter Four

"There ye are me lovelies. Smells almost like home, it does."
Aidan breathed deep and tried to relax. The smell of the plants in
this part of the ship fascinated him.

The plants were tall, gnarled thorny beasts, ugly really, but
they gave off a rich, Earthy smell that reminded him of his ship.
If he closed his eyes and conjured up a vision of one of the lush
tropical islands he'd grown up on, the plants' fragrance brought
back memories. Yes, some of it was mingled with decaying fish and
spoiled cargo, but it was a familiar, missed memory all the same.

He and his crew had often gone ashore on a small deserted strip
of island beach for hiding a bauble or two, or to enjoy a roaring
fire and a bit of rum. The drinking parties had been loud and long,
lasting for days. Afterward, several crew were somewhat worse for
the journey than Aidan would have liked as the captain, but the brief
break in the monotony of life at sea was welcome.

Aidan would could use a bit of that respite himself now.

Life on board a ship, even a floating one in the sky, made finding
time alone difficult. Especially when he didn't really want to be
alone. What he wanted was to be wrapped in Talos's arms, warm
and satisfied after yet another long and exhausting bout of mutual
exploration and discovery of their bodies and needs.

It was the 'needs' part, that growing, twisting bit of him that
demanded he be physically near Talos more and more, that had
driven Aidan to this plant room. The 'arboretum' according to Dr.

Jaclyn. Fancy name for a room full of flowers and leaves, but it made Talos, Dr. Jaclyn, and even his lordship Marius happy when he used the right words to describe his new surroundings. As if naming things with the right sounds made them familiar to him. He hadn't said it out loud, hadn't really much thought about it, but now Aidan realized it would take a long, long time before this windless, sunless, oceanless world of metal and invisible walls...*observation viewports*... would be his home.

At nine, when he'd joined his first pirate crew as cabin boy, he remembered his mother had said the center of a home was in a person's heart not where he lay his head. She had been the home in his heart until her death just before he'd set sail on his first voyage. If that remained true, his home was on board this ship because Talos was here. And *that* notion was more disturbing than comforting.

This growing, overpowering need to be with the hunter, to be touching him, kissing him, to have the great beastie's snake-like cock writhing and prodding his insides, making him moan and cry out like a man possessed by demons was...so many things. Aidan couldn't dwell on it. Not without feeling the need to run. Back on Earth, he'd have run a jolly ashore on a deserted beach, made a roaring fire of driftwood and gotten drunk.

But there was no place on board this ship to run except to this arboretum. No one else liked to come here much. Dr. Jaclyn said it was the sound of some of the plants eating the small lizard-like creatures that lived in among them that kept people away. It all sounded much like his crew snoring to Aidan. Smelled a bit like them, too.

He walked through the lush surroundings until he found the small arrangement of glittering rocks he liked to sit on at the back of the garden. They weren't like any rock he had seen before, but he guessed they came from the same foreign country the lizard-eating plants did. They glittered green, pretty enough to fetch a piece of coin for a bit of jewelry, but they had a faint, bitter smell that could be considered offensive. He doubted many women would wear a necklace made from it. Which was one of the reasons the stones were probably still here. No profit to be made in smelly gems, pretty or not.

Sitting cross-legged in the path, Aidan took two candles out of his pocket and arranged them on the glittering stone. Talos had added dozens of candles to their rooms lately. He couldn't have a roaring fire like the old days, but a bit of flame, and he could pretend.

A slight shudder disturbed the heavy air, as if someone had moved past Aidan. Superstitious to the very bone, the pirate shivered, ghosts and sirens dancing in his mind. Looking around, he called out into the silent room, "Greetin's, mate? Anyone there?" When no one answered and no one was to be seen, Adian shook his head at his own foolishness and focused on his own enjoyment again.

From his shirt's long, full sleeve, he slid out the short, slender fire starter Talos kept in the things he took planet side. Aidan thought it was magic, like so many things in this strange place, but Talos insisted it was merely a device to ignite fires, much like his pistol had been a device to shoot lead. Whatever it was, it was fast, easy and gave flame on demand every time, a flammable, invisible *gaseous* something, whatever that meant, inside of it. Aidan didn't care about the how, he just liked seeing the flame burst out of the end whenever he touched the wand's handle.

Taking a deep breath to enjoy the rich, spicy plant fragrance, Aidan pushed away the rotten egg smell from the rocks by exhaling slowly. It seemed suddenly heavier than it had during his other visits here. It was still less offensive than a ship full of unwashed men and fish in the hot Caribbean sun.

With a flourish, he used the tiny device like a sword, slicing the heavy air playfully a time or two, the folds of his sleeve billowing with each thrust and slash. He touched the starter to the candle wicks. A bright blue-yellow flame burst out the tip.

And the room exploded in a terrifying burst of light, heat and sound.

§ § § §

Bright lights, incessantly strobing across the corridor ceiling and walls bathed the arboretum entrance in a blood red hue. A putrid, green-tinged haze hung in the air, clinging to mangled arboretum doors. Bits of dust and plant matter clung to the corridor wall opposite the permanently open entrance. Heat radiated through the gaping hole, the unexpected crackle of flames sounded like maniacal laughter in the foul air.

Three of the four emergency response members, hidden in layers of safety gear and respirators, disappeared into the waiting jaws of the newly open gate to the fires of hell. One remained in the corridor moving non-essential personnel back from the danger.

"MOVE!" The roar was so deep the word was hardly intelligible, but the fierce, guttural accompanying growl and terrifying expression of the hunter did the trick anyway. Talos's rapid pace outdistanced Marius by multiple strides as he dodged running bodies, forcibly tossing aside other beings that were not agile or fast enough to clear a path for him. He barreled past the fire fighter and plunged into the arboretum, disappearing in the heavy smoke.

As Marius rounded the corner behind Talos, one of the suited responders rushed toward him to report. "Three men are inside to contain the active fire along with Lt. Kia. Sensors indict a single human life form was inside when an explosion of unknown origin ripped through the sanctuary."

"The human, Ensign Hart?" His tone told the ensign what he was really asking.

"No word yet." Hart ran beside Marius as he reported. "The fire suppressives couldn't be released without suffocating anyone inside."

"The negative pressure protocol?" It would instantaneously remove all the oxygen in the room for 3 croms, starving the fire, then reestablish a normal atmosphere immediately. Most oxygen-based creatures could easily survive the time limit.

Hart shook his head. "Sorry, sir. The door is blown out. There wasn't any way to seal it off for a vacuum to be established."

Stunned, Marius almost stopped dead, then ran faster. "How the hell did a pressure bulk door get that damaged? That's impossible."

"Don't know yet, sir. There is still an active fire in the room."

"Get engineering to bring down compression walls immediately so we can seal the room."

"Already on their way, Commander." Hart barked more orders into his comm and assigned newly arrived shipmates to contain the growing onlookers.

"And see what is keeping Medical." Not waiting for a response, Marius took a respirator from a responder. Dropping low to avoid the worst of the fumes, he entered the exotic garden. Most of the plants and insect life in this area were from the plant Solkar, a world covered with numerous noxious-smelling, ugly plants, many of them carnivorous. Yet it did have an oddly calming atmosphere according to documentation. Marius was never willing to tolerate the smell long enough to find out for himself. It existed because the space station was a base for a small colony of Solkar traders. But Marius never knew anyone beside Aidan, who frequented it. Not even the Solkars. Marius suddenly realized Aidan had found the one place on the station where he could truly be alone. And that wasn't safe for anyone.

The corridor held an ominous scent of spent sulfur and methane fumes. Fresh billows of green smoke rolled out of the savaged opening to be sucked up to the ceiling through exposed vents mightily dragging them away. Heat radiated in the rank air. The hiss of manual suppressives being used was barely audible over the snap and crackle of flames.

Suddenly a huge shadow raced toward him. Marius backed away, recognizing his friend only seconds before they would have collided. Talos carried a dark figure cradled in his arms like a small child.

A shout from behind alerted him that Ensign Hart was at his side giving the order for everyone to evacuate. Compression walls and the engineering staff were here to seal the room off and properly contain and decontaminate the entire arboretum.

He turned and followed his men out. The moment they hit the corridor, compression walls were fitted into the torn opening and activated by responders. They swelled to fit the doorway. Fire protocols instantly extinguished any active fire.

Marius got Lt. Kia's attention. "I want to know the cause of this *yesterday*, Lieutenant. Those sealant doors shouldn't be damaged like this. Find me the cause."

"Yes, Commander." Kia saluted and turned away to address his men. Marius's attention was pulled away by the sound of loud voices. Medical had arrived and it wasn't too hard to figure out who was doing the shouting.

"I can get him to sick bay faster." Talos roared, staring down Dr. Rice and half a dozen medical techs. Aidan lay motionless in the hunter's tightly clenched, muscle-bound arms. The pirate's clothes were barely there, his hair was smoking.

"Yes, but I can treat him *faster* if you just put him on the transport panel. There are things I can do here and during transport." Rice stepped forward and lowered her voice to a soft, persuasive tone. "Let me help."

"Let us help, Talos." Marius went to his friend's side and gently began disentangling Aidan from Talos' grip. He was alarmed to see panic and anger on the usually controlled hunter's face. Emotions flashed over the rigid contours of the gray flesh, each one vanishing as fast as it appeared until a calm, blank expression fell into place.

Talos moved forward and settled his lover onto the transporter bed. "He is not breathing. Hasn't been since I found him."

Stepping away, Talos pushed Aidan's hair out of his face, exposing the ashen skin and slight blue tinge to the pirate's lips as a parting gesture. He moved to one side as Rice and her assistants descended on their patient. The portable bed slid down the hall at a rapid pace, machines blinking and whistling as each new technical device was added to the man on the surface. It didn't take long for Aidan to disappear under them all.

Talos trailed after them, close, but out of the way.

Marius remained behind, drawn back to the 'accident' now that the compression walls were removed, air filtered and the fire out. This should not have been possible on his station. On any station. Arboretums didn't explode, not even Soklar ones.

Chapter Five

They entered the sick bay at a trot. More staff joined them as Rice began shouting commands for equipment and supplies. Rice bent over Aidan, examining him while some of the staff began cutting off what was left of his singed clothing. Rice listened to the pirate's chest and announced to her staff, "Get the ventilator online. Standard setup for Aidan last exam settings."

Moving into an opening between staffers, Talos caressed an unmarked side of Aidan's pale face and commanded, "You goddamn, brainless, little shit, listen to me and just breathe, Runt, just keep *breathing*."

Tubes and wires appeared and were connected to the young man. Talos moved to make room for new staff members and pieces of equipment as they all tried to save Aidan's life. Rubbing gently at an open patch of skin on Aidan's lean chest Talos made a faint clicking sound in the back of his throat. "Ti-ta, ti-ta."

Straightening, Talos demanded, "What's the lowdown, Doc? Why aren't your machines doing the job?" Aidan's chest rose and fell in a slow, regular rhythm the hunter knew was not the pirate's own. It sounded choked and tight, not at all the soft, snoring noise his lover made. "How much of a jam is he in?"

"If you mean how much trouble is Aidan having, he's having plenty. He inhaled super-heated air. He must have been fairly far—" Jaclyn Rice stopped as Marius and two armed security personnel entered the sick bay. The armed guards took up posts on either side of Aidan's bed. Rice turned a disapproving look on Marius.

"Commander, what's going on? This isn't the place for armed guards."

"I'm sorry, but it is for the time being, Doctor." Marius softened his voice and reassured her, "This wasn't an accident." He raised both hands in supplication at the doctor's attempt to protest. "Just trust me." Marius motioned for Talos to follow him to the far side of the bay, but Talos merely stared at him. Marius gave up with a small sigh. "We found an explosive had been layered between the doors. When they sealed shut, it activated."

"Don't be a stooge! Damage to the entrance was massive. If the runt had a hand in it, he would have still been by the doors. This dame would be sewing him back together from tiny pieces." Talos drew closer to Aidan, a low menacing hum encouraging the medics surrounding the bed to make a path for him.

Lights blinked and the machines regular patterns became more comforting to the hunter. Anything was better than the chaos and alarms that had been a part of his mate's previous stay in the sick bay. Even if Talos was the only one who could remember it after the time jump the Oracans had engineered to save the frustrating pirate's life. This felt like a reoccurring nightmare he was being forced to play out a second time.

"Then he didn't know about it." Ignoring the hunter's slang, Dr. Rice injected Aidan with a gentle nudge of a pencil thin injector. An oxygen sensor gradually stopped flashing. The sound of Talos taking a deep breath was audible over the thrum of the medical equipment and staff. Rice pointed at two of her staff saying, "Irrigate his eyes and decontaminate him using protocol twelve, immediately." She stepped away, drawing Marius and Talos with her to let her people work and give their patient some privacy.

"You're sure?" Marius pressed for more details.

"Security sent their report to me just now so we have the list of toxic and non-toxic elements present in the room. All of them are irritating Aidan's lung tissue. Not surprising, most of them are present naturally on Soklar. They're unpleasant to most humans, apparently pirates not being a part of that affected population, but none of them cause respiratory damage like this. Not on their own, anyway."

"What's the score then? Heal him. He's suffering." Talos longed to touch his mate's pale face, but didn't risk interrupting the nurses working on the unconscious pirate.

"That may not be so easy. He's has been exposed to a rare element." Rice paused to take a hesitant breath. "One that shouldn't be there. Or anywhere else where human life is found."

Marius tapped a nearby monitor that connected him to the main computer. "Lt. Kia reports the explosion was a compound of meleca and kazelc-12." He looked up from the screen to catch Talos's attention. "Isn't kazelc-12 only found on Oracan?"

"Yeah. And meleca is largely mined on the neighboring planet of Sblo." Talos fought back the urge to smash his fist into a solid surface. "It looks like my family snag is coming to me instead of waiting for me to come it."

Rice frowned, but stayed focused on her patient. "Well, the combination of the Soklar plants gases and both explosive elements created a third byproduct. It's known as nitrogenamine-B. In humans it causes bleeding and blistering in lung tissue. It damages mucous membranes, causing swelling. That's why he's having difficulty breathing. His lungs are swollen, air is being trapped, making it hard to exhale. The medication I just gave him is helping. He's stable for the moment. I'm hoping the tissue replicators work for him. We'll know soon enough." She paused, then added, "For some reason, I-I don't have a lot of confidence in them with Aidan." Her brow knitted together for a moment, her expression puzzled, as if she was trying to remember something just out of reach. "I don't *know* why, I just *feel* it." Shaking her head and shoulders as if she could actually shed the odd feeling, she turned away. "Never mind, it's ridiculous. I'll let you know when I have medical evidence of Aidan's response."

Talos pretended not to hear her. He wasn't going to reveal a memory she shouldn't have anymore. He knew what needed to be done. The dame and all her shiny equipment wasn't going to give Aidan what he needed.

But right now, his number one need was to find the threat on board this station in the *real* present time. "Meleca and kazelc-12 are stable compounds by themselves. It takes someone who knows the jive to mix them into a firecracker big enough to blow those doors."

"I'm reviewing the security footage from earlier for any sightings of Aidan. Look at this." Marius keyed the monitor and a muted, short conversation between the pirate and another man filled the screen. Marius froze it when Aidan swaggered away. "That's Opius Worth. Security is looking for him along with this man." Marius activated the screen and showed Worth joined by another, rougher looking man. They followed after Aidan, but were lost in the tangle of people in the shopping atrium. "The security footage outside the arboretum has been tampered with. Either by the explosion or design. Worth registered as a private colony entrepreneur when he boarded. A little investigation of his history shows his real profession is conning unsuspecting investors out of their credits with nothing to show for it." Marius flicked a hand and his screen ran through Worth's history. He stopped at the most recent entry. "Guess what his last project was? Delivering minerals from Oracan to Miniso."

"Colonies like Miniso use kazelc-12 to filter their water supply." Talos tapped Worth's image on the monitor. "It gets worse. Never met the thug, but I know the name. There's a price on Worth's head." He reassured the suddenly startled commander. A Hunt was no small matter. "No, not an Oracan Hunt, just a rumor around. Gambling debts to someone with clout. The juice is adding up and he can't pay."

"Maybe that's why he's here. I can think of worse places to hide. P6 is secure, but we're still out of mainstream travel. If he'd stayed low key and didn't cause any trouble, he might have avoided recognition for a long while."

"Maybe, but he singled Aidan out. You can see he was waiting for him. He's a fingerman. It wasn't a chance hook up. I recognize the dodge. He wanted the runt. Aidan sensed it and went on the lam like the smart, little pirate he is." Sudden raised voices pulled Talos's attention back to the sick bay bed.

Aidan was thrashing on the bed, arms tangled with several

medical technicians as they tried to keep him from pulling at the airway enhancer in his mouth. His eyes were wide open, frantic, pupils so large they looked black.

"You're safe, Aidan. You're safe. Leave the breather in. You've been hurt, but you'll be all right." Dr. Rice's cool, reassuring tone meant to calm Aidan seemed to produce the opposite effect on the pirate.

Talos knew Aidan hated that tone of voice from the doctor. Whatever the dame found reasonable in the sick bay was sure to mean discomfort and loss of something the pirate valued. So far, he had lost his precious long hair, his clothes, and a bag of glorious, pilfered gems to her helpful hands. The dame wasn't going to calm his mate. Only he could do that now. He felt the biological snare tighten within him, overpowering and insistent.

The hunter strode to the bedside. The barricade of bodies parted before him like a well-rehearsed sports play. Marius joined Rice on the opposite side of the bed. Rice looked tired and worried.

Talos took both of the thin wrists in his fists, instantly stilling the frantic struggles. "I'm here, runt. Behave." Rubbing gently at a bruise forming on Aidan's cheek, Talos made a faint clicking sound in the back of his throat. Aidan focused on the hunter, his rapid heart rate slowed, and the terror left his eyes. Alarms stopped buzzing and the pirate's breathing seemed to ease. Clearly surprised, Rice frowned at the Hunter, but he ignored her and continued to make the faint 'ta-ti' noise over and over again.

Marius watched his friend for several heartbeats, then looked around him at the rushed staff and Rice's increasingly drawn expression. "How is he?"

"Better." She gave him a weak smile then looked back at Aidan. "Improving, he's much better, but there *is* a problem."

Rice watched as Talos tenderly ran a soothing hand through the pirate's hair, still occasionally making the 'ta-ti' clicking noise, ignoring everyone else in the room. "He's not responding to the tissue regeneration like he should be. It worked perfectly when he first arrived on this station, but it can't seem to syn with his DNA structure completely for some reason now. I can't understand it. His cell structure is slightly changed. And changed in a way the regenerator isn't calibrated to handle. He's also running a fever I can't find a cause for. I've never seen anything like it before."

Talos pulled his gaze away from Aidan for a brief moment to stare at Rice. "In what way?" There was that time loop feeling again. Did he really have to say this out loud again? Explain to that dame he was the cause of the problem?

Rice pointed at the regeneration device strapped to Aidan's chest. "Seven hundred years of evolution between Aidan's time and ours has produced a difference in our DNA structure. It may explain why he can touch you and other humans can't, but it doesn't explain this now. The cell regen worked before and it should now." She looked helpless and frustrated. "He's changed significantly, and that change is affecting my ability to heal him and I have no idea why."

Talos turned his attention back on his lover, his mate for life.

Marius pressed a comforting hand to Rice's shoulder. "So what do we do?"

Rice looked at a readout monitor a nurse handed her and shook her head. The nurse silently left. "I'm working on it, but I'm sorry, until I can figure out the needed changes for the recalibration, I'm at a loss."

Okay, so he *was* going to have to have that conversation again. Even if no one but he remembered it, it was still irritating to have to take the doctor's gaff a second time. God damned dames! "I'm the source of Aidan's problem. I did this to him."

"How?" He really couldn't tell which one had spoken first, Marius or Rice. They spit out their disbelief in unison. They spent way too much time together.

Talos gripped his mate's cool hand, his piercing gaze locked with Aidan's dark, wide open stare like a lifeline. Runt might as well know about it now, it was as good as any other time. "Oracans take a mate for life." He really didn't want to discuss Oracan biology with outsiders. He lowered his voice and studied his mate's reactions. It was easier than seeing Marius' flustered expression or the doctor's disapproving glare. "And when we mate, our body fluids are absorbed by our partner's body. Our chemistry blends and the partners are marked for life as belonging to the other by their scent, their taste, all of it. Their blood is joined. But that's between two Oracans. I didn't know it would happen to Aidan. No Oracan has ever mated with a human before. No human has been able to tolerate the touch of a Oracan, let alone mate with them." Talos glanced at Rice, including Marius in the flickering look. "No one but Oracan is permitted to have biological data on my race. You know that, Doc. And that's what you're going to need to fix him. Because, now, he's part Oracan, too."

"Let me send a call for assistance to the Oracan Council. Surely they would be willing to share information if it meant a life was at stake? The 'mate'," she said it with just a hint of disapproval, "of one of their own celebrated Hunters!"

"You don't know Oracan culture very well, Doctor."

"Seriously, Jaclyn, Oracans do not share technology of *any* kind. They share nothing except their skill and reputations as bounty hunters and diplomats. And that is shared only with a full council vote at a lengthy formal trial. There is no way they will share medical technology or even basic biological data. Many a diplomat and corporation has tried and failed."

"We'll just see about that. I'm not without my own persuasive powers and reputation." Rice did a rapid visual check of the monitors and left for her office, head held high and mouth set in a determined line.

Talos stared at the now sleeping pirate as a new realization hit him in the gut. His race's genetic mandate had forced him to bond—for the first time in all of Oracan history—with a human, someone outside his species. And for what? So that the bond could be the cause of Aidan's death? Was it some grand predestined joke to deter others from the same course? How could that be when he was dragged into the bond by his Oracan physiology. He hadn't been able to resist Aidan. Maybe this was why it was called a 'genetic snare" to begin with, maybe he wasn't the first. Maybe others hadn't survived and had been erased from his culture's history.

"Bonding. Love. Whatever." He smoothed a wayward strand of hair from his pirate's face and tried to hide his grimace in a reassuring growl. "Ain't that just grand."

Chapter Six

Talos had stayed with Aidan until the pirate improved enough that the breather was removed. His lover was sleeping, if restless, under the doctor's medically forced unconsciousness. The young man had jerked and twitched as if he were fighting off an entire wave of enemies. Talos had realized he was re-enacting his last fight to the death before his life had been stolen and his entire world changed.

Taking advantage of the peaceful period, Talos returned to the privacy of their living quarters to make an important communication.

"I've been informed your lovely Dr. Rice is trying to unravel the mystery of Aidan's unprecedented physiological changes with formal requests for Oracan medical research from our Council." Talos's brother Zeban filled the communication screen.

"She isn't mine. She's Marius's problem, the poor palooka." Talos grunted, a small sound of regret for his friend's taste in woman. Dr. Jaclyn Rice was brilliant, beautiful, dedicated and thorny as hell to deal with. For some reason she disliked bounty hunters, especially ones that captured then mated with their prey. Dames.

"So the doc is hitting up the Council?"

"She is. And rather insistently, I might add. She is a forceful female."

"What can I say, humans are a feisty race. And the dame likes the Runt." He shook his head at the memory of the latest yapping she had done over his refusal to remove the bounty band from Aidan's wrist. For a right babe, she didn't understand a hunter's world or the constant dangers in it. "Acts like she gave birth to him sometimes."

"No matter what anyone's personal feelings are for Aidan, all Oracan medical information is restricted from off-worlders."

"Zeban, Aidan is changing. He's better, but he needs help. What happens when he gets hurt?"

"Afraid he won't be up to the…exhausting challenges of the bond, brother?"

"Butt out."

"Don't be offended. I'm enjoying seeing you immersed on a personal level that doesn't involve the business of stalking a new prey. It's good to see you rejoin life again, Talos. You have been too distant from our family since our youngest brother's death. If for no other reason than he has awakened your need for companionship, I welcome your little human into our family cashe."

"Well, if you want to keep him there, the doc needs that information in case something happens to him like the last time. The medical equipment still doesn't recognize his altering cellular base anymore. If he gets seriously injured, she won't be able to help him much."

"There are limitations to what medical information can be shared, brother. Your pirate is the first outside species to mate with ours. It's unprecedented. There are no rules to govern Dr. Rice's requests. I'm doubtful the Council will approve them, Talos."

"So you're just going to wash your hands of him?"

"I'm reminding you, Aidan isn't your official mate until you both complete the bonding ritual. Here on Oracan."

"What's that got to do with anything?"

"Actually, I'm telling you as your *brother*, that once Aidan is *officially* an Oracan mate, there may be grounds to appeal a decision made to deny the exchange of medical information. After all, I imagine Oracan researchers will be interested in obtaining Dr. Rice's finds in return."

"So you think if Aidan passes the challenges and completes the rituals, the Council will have no choice but to cooperate?" It was hard to keep a note of hope out of his voice.

"Oracans take care of their own." Zeban grew quieter, patience and sympathy gentling his words. "Once your sly, little pirate achieves mate status by our own rules, he will be considered not only a Son of Menalon, but a Oracan citizen with all responsibilities and rights."

"You're being square with me on this?" Zeban was offering a thin but pragmatic lifeline. "You think the Council will bend?"

"The Council prides themselves on being adaptable and forward thinking. If presented with evidence that you and Aidan have bonded by ritual, there will be little choice in the matter."

"Aidan is clever and wily, but he's still human, Zeban. The ritual is difficult even for Oracans. Only the strongest and most cunning are permitted to bond and breed."

"Breeding's not an issue here, but I suspect he's feeling the rising draw of the sexual aspects of the bond or our doctor wouldn't be looking so hard for medical information."

"He's handling that part. *We're* handling it."

"If you both pass the rites of bonding, your little human will be free of the worst of the effects. There is no disputing that. Where is he now, Talos? Asleep? Or unconscious after a marathon bout of mating? How long do you think he'll last as the urges continue to rise?"

"The ritual would take away the hunger?"

"Only the part of it caused by the bonding fever. The ritual will serve two purposes, Talos. Dissolve the fever and solidify his standing as a Oracan. You need both of them."

"Both ways, he's protected."

"Yes, but don't expect it to be easy, either." Zeban let out a long, slow breath. "I suspect there will be challengers. I suspect Chakki to object. She has wanted an offspring from the cashe for some time now."

"If there isn't a bond, it can't happen. And there wasn't. She knows that. I completed the challenge. She did not."

"I'm sure she will allow you to explain that fact to her, again, in person. Keep in mind there are forces at work right now that do not want the Cashe of Menalon to succeed. At anything."

"Let them challenge us. Aidan is more warrior than any number of our kinsmen."

Zeban smiled, silently agreeing and apparently pleased. "Then it's settled. I can make arrangements for the ritual now." Zeban shifted restlessly in his chair and cleared his throat. "I'll send you a message when all is in place."

"Honor and compassion, my brother." Talos gave the usual salutation and reached for the button to disconnect.

§ § § §

"Now that he's good enough to travel, it's the only way to fix things." Talos rammed a few bits of cloth and leather into a small satchel. A mired of weapons—knives, prongs, battle axes, and two very ornate, curved blades were rolled into a small carpet-like carrying case and tossed beside the full satchel. "So save your breath, Doc. We're going."

"He's not strong enough."

"You released him, said he was jake!"

"I never said he was…whatever that means. I said he was good enough to be released from the sick bay. Not to go participate in a barbaric battle for his life on a barren, hostile planet against a race of trained kill—" She paused, lips pursed in the effort. "*Bounty hunters*, who are three times his size and four times as deadly."

Aidan was right. Her green eyes really did flash like lightning when she was japping at the top of her lungs. He'd never noticed before. Talos growled softly, casting a glance at his mate lounging on the edge of a tabletop, boots swinging in time to a beat only the pirate could hear. "We'll handle it."

"*We?* Are you going to be in the challenge with him? Beside him all the way, helping him?"

"No." Every muscle wanted to snap tight. He worked at keeping his posture loose and natural, but he couldn't stop his nostrils from flaring, scenting the room to draw in as much of his lover's essence as he could to fight off the memories. "My trials will be spiritual. His will be physical."

"Marius, tell your thick-headed friend you support your Chief Medical Officer's professional opinion." Rice crossed her arms and glared at all three of them, daring anyone of them to dismiss her.

Her shoulders slumped in defeat when the commander shook his head, saying, "I support my medical officer to the fullest, but this is Aidan's decision and his alone. He's an adult, even if it's hard to recognize that fact most of the time."

"Aye, gov. Me'self is all for it." Aidan jumped off the tabletop and swaggered to a rumpled shirt laying on a chair. He wandered over to Talos's packed satchel and stuffed the shirt into an open corner. "There, all sorted out." He grinned at Rice then winked at his lover. "Never passed by a bit of sport or a voyage to a foreign land in me life!"

"All right! I concede." Rice crossed her arms over her chest. "You're both going to Oracan to put your lives at risk." Rice stepped in front of Talos when he made a move to grab his parcels. "It's only been one day since the attack. He needs rest not challenges." Stony silence greeted her attempt at persuasion. "Okay. You will let me know if he needs anything, especially if the Council grants a sharing of medical information? He's still battling a fever."

"It's a bonding fever." Frustration was clear in his voice. "It's natural."

She shot back, "Not for humans."

"The healers on Oracan can handle it."

Wordlessly, she stepped closer, risking touching him, a steely glint in those lightning green eyes again.

Talos let a big breath out, long and slow. "If you're needed, I'll get on the horn to Marius."

Her gaze darted to the commander. "He means he'll call." Marius placed his hand on her folded arms and gently drew her out of the hunter's path.

"No need to worry your fiery head, me lady. I be fit as a bowman's fiddle. Been needing an outing like this. Feel the sand under me boots and the wind against me flesh again. A stiff breeze always cools the sweat from a man's brow." Aidan wiped his cheek with the sleeve of his shirt and slipped away from Rice's attempt to touch his overly pink, damp forehead. He tugged at the weapon sash belted over Talos's broad chest. "Let's be off, my great, gray beast, afore the tide turns and we lose the wind at our backs."

"That doesn't affect galactic ships." Talos gathered up their belongings for the trip and followed his anxious lover out the door.

"Course it does. No ship sails without wind. Not seeing it 'cause it be *wind*, luv." Aidan looked over his shoulder at Dr. Rice and Marius's unsettled expressions. "'Sides, be a storm brewing aft. No need to secure the hatches if a body's not in it."

Aidan bestowed a fevered, but grand, smile on his lover. "Put an eye to the horizon, shall we?"

Chapter Seven

The late evening Oracan sky reminded Aidan of the rich velvet cloaks worm by the more prosperous English gentlemen travelers that he had stolen from at one time or another in pirate raids on unfortunate merchant ships. Deep orange, streaked with copper bands, the sky sparkled with a dense dusting of hazy lights, not unlike the diamonds that shone brightly in the bag of gems Aidan had liberated from his long lost and still hidden treasure.

That was where any similarity to Aidan's old life and Earth ended.

The planet was hot. And brilliant, blindingly so, as if those diamonds in the sky had rained down silver dust from their shoulders and covered every crusty rock and stretch of sand with their riches. It was almost too glorious to take in.

Aidan jumped from Talos's ship to the landing pad outside the Oracan Council chambers then strode off the smooth surface's edge to kick the sparkling dust into the dry, scorching air. It swirled briefly in a light breeze, covering the toes of his boots with a pale-yellow film that looked like powdered gold.

"Diamonds glitterin' above 'n gold dust under me boots." He called out to his lover as the hunter stood patiently by the ship, waiting. Aidan grabbed a handful of yellow sand and let it flow through his fingers like water to the ground. "Like it already, Talos."

"You'll get plenty of time to enjoy it. Scram back over here." Talos nodded toward a silent, waiting group of Oracans. "Council is waiting to greet you."

"Ah, a welcoming party." Aidan eyed the group suspiciously. Some wore the long colorful robes like Talos's brother. He picked Zeban's distinct presence out of the crowd as the only face he recognized. Several others were dressed as his hunter, barely clothed, weapons heavy, all muscle bound and towering.

He wasn't a hundred percent sure, but he thought there was at least one lass in the group. One had a more delicate curve to their features and shoulders that were slightly less broad than all the others. Only slightly. Maybe it was just a skinny Oracan? Or the heat of the planet blurring his vision. It was hard to focus that far away. The intense heat shimmered up from every surface around them, dry and brittle. The group suddenly wavered, melting into a swirl of various colors and disapproving frowns.

He felt the air rush around him, scalding his skin, then the abrupt assurance of Talos's body pressed to his, steadying him in place. A small shake and a deep, wordless murmur put the alien world back right side up. "Just need me land legs back."

Aidan widened his eyes and blinked, hoping to push away the blurriness. He was only partially successful. Straightening his spine, he grinned at his mate and whispered, "A boarding party on dry land." His hand fell to his waist to land on the hilt of one of the small ornate blades the hunter had packed. Talos had secured one in his own sash then given the other to him just before disembarking the ship. Aidan loved the weight of it on him and the way it drew his body heat into itself. He was feeling more at home with every passing moment. Except, maybe for this. "Does *not* bode well for any pirate, luv. Savvy?" He allowed himself to lean into his lover for a moment, drawing confidence and strength from being so close to the hulking beast of his desires.

"I savvy. No bloodshed before the formal greetings." Aidan noticed how Talos kept himself between him and, if the number of hands that rested on a weapon hilt was anything to go by, the mostly hostile onlookers.

"Ta'fore, but not aft'?" He pushed reluctantly away, swaying just a little before regaining his balance. He consciously kept a finger hooked into the edge of the hunter's sash as an anchor. Let the gray beasts think what they like. Talos was his and he was laying claim to him.

"After, anything goes, runt."

"Then let's not keep the monstrous brethren waiting."

Halfway across the open stretch between them and the waiting horde, Aidan released his finger grip on the hunter. His palms itched for a new bauble or two. Maybe those voluminous robes had pockets to plunder. Gods knew the hunters had so little on he could see they hid nothing worth coin anywhere he was willing to reach into. If he was forced to run their savage gauntlet to claim his hunter, the least they could allow him was a sovereign or two.

Talos led him directly to the older male beside his brother. Talos bowed to the Council member, his right fist placed over his mid-abdomen then he slid it up his body until it covered his heart in the millennia-old tradition of his race. "Honor and compassion, High Principle Belith."

Belith, Zeban and all the Oracans returned the gesture as one. "Honor and compassion." These were more than mere words to these people. They were a declaration of what their race held in the highest of regard—their personal and racial honor, and their responsibility to regard each situation or being with compassion. Aidan knew from firsthand experience, Oracan compassion could be a harsh gift.

His mate had grown quieter with each stride toward the circle of Oracans, his step stronger, his breathing more controlled, his scent so intense Aidan found himself drawing in deeper breaths to capture the heady aroma. His cock jerked to life and fought for room to expand, making walking an exotic dance of its own.

He noticed several of the hunters take a step back as they thankfully stopped in front of the Councilmen, their nostrils flaring and eyes narrowed on many of them. Aidan suddenly realized every one of them had detected the pairs' explosively intimate bond.

The pirate shoved away a moment of embarrassment as the public knowledge of his sexual relationship with another male washed over the group of strangers. It wasn't a hanging offense anymore. It wasn't even noteworthy to anyone beside himself. A surge of pride replaced the shame. Talos stood, as a solitary hunter, before all of his people to claim his right to mate with a person outside their kind. They weren't hostile because he was a man, it was because he was human. Outsider. *Offworlder,* they called it here.

Aidan was just beginning to understand how incredibly brave the hunter was to expose himself, and Aidan, to this Council and their Ceme magic rituals. His resolve to win this much talked about ceremony deepened. He'd fought soldiers and pirates alike, savage cannibals from faraway lands, drunken brawlers, and frenzied sharks. Surely a tribe of alien lizard men wouldn't be that much harder. He hoped. He needed the edge of surprise with this lot.

"Ahoy, kin and brethren of me own great beastly hunter, Tals of Menalon." Caressing the fancy blade hilt for reassurance, Aidan gave a grand bow then grinned at each of the welcoming party. Sweat rolled down his temples. The growing heat of his own flesh was cooled by the trickle of liquid until the dry wind vanquished it to whatever hellfire the brittle air had blown in from.

The world wavered a bit. His chest hurt and the heavy air felt like sand in his lungs. His smile widened and he made a show of flipping his beaded hair, letting the miserably short strands fall into his face, hoping to shield all those prying eyes from seeing the pain tightening across his drawn, sweaty face. "Aidan Maymon, freeman and once captain of the legendary *Jamaican Maid.* Me'selfs pleased to make your acquaintance."

"Welcome, Aidan of Maymon. I am Belith, High Principle of the Council of Oracan." Belith murmured in his deep, cutting voice then he added, "The Council is gratified your hunter has claimed his right to the bonding ritual." He then turned to Zeban to continue the greeting, apparently content to step back and observe. Aidan was sure the official's nose was going to walk off his face as his nostrils flared repeatedly like an exotic belly dancer's hips.

"Talos of Menalon, brother of mine." Zeban tilted his head in acknowledgment of their family link. "All is in place for the ritual challenge to begin at nightfall." He gave his attention back to Aidan. "Allow me to introduce the others who have chosen to show witness to your mating ritual." Zeban gestured at each individual in the small crowd. He started with the robed Oracan beside him. "Our brother, High Principle Arco, and," he indicated the male to Arco's right, shorter than the other three brothers with a dour expression mismatched with kind violet eyes, "Wacad, a healer, and a brother."

The Council members' robes left their left shoulder exposed and Aidan could see the dark tattoos that adored every Oracan there, even the female. They varied from one bulging, muscular body to the next, but it was easy to see that unlike the rest, Talos, Zeban, Arco and Wacad bore the exact same markings on their left shoulders. He guessed it was much like shipmates getting the same ink to commemorate a good raiding party or the sinking of a vile, British vessel.

"Four of ya?" Aidan leered at Talos. "Mum and Da musta been amorous lovebirds, eh?" He tried unsuccessfully to shift his now painful erection to a more comfortable position by swaying his hips. When that didn't work, he turned his back to the group, swiftly freed his shaft from the fold of pants cloth it had uncurled into, tucked it to one side and swung back around as if nothing had happened. No one's expression had changed, but the air was heavy with the evidence of sex and sweat.

"Must be that devilish spell yo'uns call the 'snare'." He put out a hand to steady himself against Talos. It looked like nothing more than an intimate touch, but a strong wave of dizziness had suddenly rocked him. The heat was growing unbearable. "Understand completely, mate."

Aidan hesitated for a moment, then forced himself to focus on the healer. "Healer? Another sawbones. Dr. Jaclyn wants ta discuss potions an' such with the likes of you, sir." He waggled a finger in Wacad's direction. "But be careful, mate. She's a beauty, but she'll gnaw a man's ear off with chatter if given the chance."

Aidan swayed as he twisted away. Talos steadied him, leaning down to catch the hoarse whisper Aidan spoke into his chest. "Not feelin' so fine, luv. Think we can hurry along the greetings an' such?"

"Can you manage for the count of two hundred?" Croms and

decas, the way time was measured in this current century, meant nothing to the pirate yet. Talos usually demanded Aidan adapt to all the ways of current life. Aidan realized he must be in pretty bad shape if the merciless hunter was giving him leeway. It was important the mate of a famous hunter be strong and able. Doubly so if he was human. "Then we'll breeze outta here."

Aidan nodded but couldn't resist verbalizing the direction his thoughts really headed. "Could use a *breeze*, luv. Just a wee one. Heats a bit much, don't you think?"

Gently pushing his mate away, Talos stayed close. After a quick glance at Zeban and Belith, both of whom gave him an almost imperceptible nod, he addressed the attentively watching group. "I, Talos of Menalon, Oracan Hunter, present my chosen life mate, Aidan of Maymon, human pirate." A fierce glare dared anyone to object. Several shifted their gaze away, but none spoke. Talos let the silence drag out then added, "Your witness to our bonding is welcome, whatever the nature."

The next few moments were a blur to Aidan. He nodded and smiled through introductions as Zeban presented each new Oracan. Chakki, the female Aidan had picked out of the crowd, was a high Principle Council member. She greeted Talos warmly, for an Oracan, raking an assessing glance over the pirate while worming her way into an invitation to dinner and the bonding ceremony. *Bloody toff.* He could tell it was difficult for Zeban to deflect her determination. Talos seemed disinterested and distant to her, but he didn't voice any objection. *Clever one, she was. High an' mighty, too.*

A large Oracan, Stol, neither dressed as a hunter or diplomat, was introduced as a son of another High Principle. He had what the pirate pegged as shifty eyes, and a slight twitch to his body. Aidan could read tension and indecision in every restless wiggle of fingers, each hooded glance and dark stare aimed at him and his lover. Stol disliked Aidan and feared Talos. He didn't need to be able to smell things like an Oracan to discover that. He put Stol on his list to watch closely.

One Oracan seemed overly brash, nearly elbowing Stol aside to step close to Aidan. He proclaimed himself to be Jak, Oracan hunter and challenger. That proclamation caused the talons on the backs of Talos's arms to fully extend as a reflexive response to Jak's aggressive challenge. Even Aidan could smell the hunter, a rank, heavy musk that reminded the pirate of the filthiest brothels in the poorest ports. One low, humming growl from Talos was answered by a similar sound from Jak, but Aidan felt his hunter's hum ripple through his body on the shimmering waves of heat in the air. It blocked out the sudden spike of fear he felt from challenger's eager, hard stare. *Death threats on introduction. Ah, well, a pirate's life 'twas a same everywhere. Number two on my watch list.*

Talos was less guarded with the last greeter. Dagi was part of the Council's staff, head of security. He was present to escort them back to Talos's father's cashe. There had been attempts on the elder's life and family. Dagi was tasked with keeping the ritual safe for everyone. Aidan felt an obvious dislike from the guard, but he wasn't sure if it was directed at him or Talos. Dagi seemed to have enough hateful glares for them both. *Bloody hell! Just watch out for 'em all.*

"All ruddy cutthroats, the lot of them. Feelin' right at home here, luv." The count to two hundred ended and with it went Aidan's preciously held stamina. He grabbed at Talos's weapons sash as his body melted into a puddle of sweaty flesh on the dusty, yellow sand. The boiling heat, and everything else, blissfully disappeared.

Chapter Eight

"It isn't lack of compassion, Talos. It's law. We do not share our biological data. No one outside our race is permitted that knowledge." Arco paced the anteroom open to the treatment room where Wacad meticulously examined the unconscious, little human under Talos's long distance glare. "There would be untold chaos in the galaxy. Our time traveling is ours alone. No other race can duplicate it. We've proven that in all the relocation studies over millennia."

Zeban and Arco were the only others in the medical suite besides Talos, Wacad and Aidan.

Zeban earnestly echoed Arco's words. "It would be a pointless activity, but Oracans *would* be hunted for experimentation, exploited for personal gain, dissected, eaten, bought and sold like cargo. It can't happen."

"I thought you were on my side!" Talos ground out the words slowly. "Then don't share it. Just allow our healers to treat him. He's in a jam. Help him hold back the fever long enough to smash the ritual."

"Impossible. He's *gutleug*," Arco spit the guttural syllables out like poison. "Offworlder."

"I never knew you to be a xenophobe, bro." Talos turned to face his two siblings, talon tips rising against the surface of his now dark gray skin. "Is that what's eating you? The great house of Menalon might have to accept an offworlder into the cashe?" Talons broke through the skin, gleaming white against his gray flesh. "Or maybe because he's claimed bounty. If that's the rumble around here, he wears my band. Every chump and thug knows what a hunter's band means. Even offworlders."

"Prejudice against a species contaminating ours is not my objection, little brother." Arco rested a hand on Talos's shoulder. "Bonding with Oracans might not be biologically possible. What then? You could lose your mate to the ritual. My concern is *for* the tiny human."

"A little late." Talos closed his eyes and drew a deep breath. "He's not human anymore."

Neither Arco nor Zeban was easily startled but the confession gave both of them pause. Before they found their tongues, another voice filled the void.

"That's not precisely correct." Wacad had left Aidan's side and was standing in the wide arched doorway, quiet and watchful. All three brothers focused on him now. "He'll always be human, Talos. But…his cell structure is changing. That's the cause of his high fever. It's not tradition bonding fever. It's a human reaction. Areas of his body that produce human blood cells are altering. The extreme cellular activity is producing heat. Thus, fever."

"Altering? Why? We haven't shared blood yet. That's why we're here."

"I can't be sure, this was just a cursory examination." The healer motioned them to follow him back to Aidan's bedside. "I've re-hydrated him. Humans loose fluids very fast. He'll have to be careful of that while he's here. Fluids brought down his fever quite a bit. He needs to rest until the meal. After that, he should be as fit for the ritual as any human ever will be." Wacad cast an appraising glance over the sleeping man. "What about you?"

"Me?"

"We can smell his scent on you, see the fever burning in your veins. The snare is already tightening within you." Wacad's kind eyes studied Talos. "What will you do if your precious, little human fails?"

"He won't."

"That's a lot of trust to put in one small, strange creature, brother."

"Aidan a right guy. Fast, strong, clever. He's battled for his life before."

"And won?"

"All but once." Talos was defiant, but he got his brother's point.

"He lost to an Oracan hunter then." Arco pointed out the obvious. "He'll be facing several tonight."

"He'll make it."

"He's very small." Even Zeban, who Talos knew supported the ritual, couldn't help but voice concern. "Does he know what to expect?"

"Know right enough, m'lordship." The pirate lay sprawled on the bed, beads bright against the pillow, his tanned skin returned to a dry glow, eyes closed and chest rising in a regular rhythm. He was the picture of sleep, but Talos had known better. He'd sensed his heartrate increase several moments ago. "Small, but 'm nimble, guvs."

Aidan pushed himself up to a sitting position, testing his sense of balance was intact before sliding off the bed. "Does every cold-hearted beast on this glorious fire island desire me 'ead? Is no one friend of the family? Not even the family?"

"The runt has a point, Zeban. Is everyone in the Council against our bonding?"

"Not everyone, no. Some Council members argue it will open more relations with humans. A diplomatic step forward in balancing the Terran objections to our hunts." Zeban smiled and added, "It really doesn't matter if others are against it." He titled his head toward the awakening pirate, the ridges along his brow arching up. "Menalon has given his blessing."

Before Talos could react to the news his father had given his powerful house's approval on their unlikely pairing, Aidan drew his attention with a sway of his slender, unclothed hips. Talos's sexual responses to his chosen lover burned bright in an instant. The pirate rubbed his eyes and stretched his naked body like a cat waking from a nap, oblivious to his audience. He no longer sported a full erection, but his cock was attempting to stir and return to its earlier rigid state. He locked a heated gaze on Talos and began to walk to him. His move came to a halt when his discarded shirt sailed through the air and landed on his face.

"No time for it, runt. Put on your glad rags. We gotta a shingdig to hit."

§ § § §

The journey to Menalon's cashe was brief. The trip accomplished with a series of high speed transports and small moving discs that Aidan had to stand on. Talos occupied the same disc with him to pilot the flying platform, and Aidan soaked up as much of the hunter's scent and warmth that he could. His lover's nearness soothed his worries and preoccupied his racing thoughts. He needed his wits about him if he was going to be able to come back to this hulking beast in one piece. Or a piece that could be sufficiently mended.

Oracan homes were located deep within the mountains like caves. This shielded the population from the extreme heat, and tempered the arid atmosphere. But they were not primitive spaces. The very best in technology transformed the caves into high tech, sparse, but comfortable, elegant homes.

Menalon's chambers were among the grandest, Aidan supposed. The head of the cashe was obviously well respected by the weight the mention of his name carried with the non-family members at the first gathering. He knew his hunter had come from a powerful tribe. Dr. Rice's little nurse Amy had been very talkative about his captor's history during the pirate's time in the sick bay. Aidan was sure she was just sorry for cutting his hair off, but he'd listened and asked questions. The lass knew only what she could research on the thick glass paper thingies they used. Yes, his mate was from power and wealth. But that pesky thing about honor and compassion was annoying.

"Don't jaw at my father until he gives you the high sign. It's a respect thing. Just follow my lead." Pressed against the hunter's chest, Aidan stared up into violet eyes, eyes as bright as the finest gemstones from any foreign land. They were as full of want and need as he had ever seen them. But now, Aidan suspected, under all the simmering sexual tension was a new anxiety. The challenge of earning the respect of a powerful man that carried meaning for the hunter.

Unlike Aidan's father, who had disappeared at sea long before his son could get to know him, Talos's father had produced a gaggle of sons, who all respected and seemed to care for him. He had heard a story or two in the bars about a young Talos who had spent time on old space freighters with his father, learning English from salvaged gangster movies from early Earth. Early to Talos, future Earth for Aidan. It got confusing at times.

"Promise to toe the line, luv. Decided to think of your da as a magistrate and 'm intent on not wearing a noose."

"That'll work. Try not to yammer. He likes action over words."

"A man after me own heart then." Aidan slipped a hand between them and stroked his cock. It responded instantly, and Talos's nostrils flared. "Just need a yank an' a grope to settle me nerves." He rubbed a check over Talos's chest, nudging the sensitive plates until the hunter growled and hummed.

"That should do it." He immediately stopped both actions, enjoying the frustrated frown his lover gave him.

Anymore conversation was halted by their arrival at a large slab of polished rock the size of a boulder. It was as black as a moonless night, with veins of gold and silver running through it. It slid out of the way, revealing a cavernous entry as soon as the five of them stepped off the transport discs. Zeban lead the way and they all entered the chambers in single file, Aidan tucked in between Arco and Talos.

The silence of the room was complete. Aidan imaged it was what being swallowed by a whale must be like. The absence of the waves splashing, wind blowing through the sails, or the cry of the seagulls. Here there wasn't the light raspy sound of his own and his companion's breathing. Even the others' robes were silent, the swish of fabric and the tap of footsteps snatched out of the very air. It was as if the chamber had devoured them.

"Greetings. I am Pena. Please follow." A female Oracan appeared out of a side alcove, delivering the traditional Oracan salute. "Honor and compassion." All four brothers returned the greeting.

Pena was tall and fierce, and very much like Chakki. She flashed a hostile look toward Aidan, but it settled on Talos and stayed there. Talos endured it, but then lowered his gaze. Not until then did the female look away.

"Menalon awaits his sons." She gestured to a room to the right. "The ritual meal is to begin." There was a little too much venom in the word 'ritual'. Talos stiffened, but Zeban made a low sound and Pena bowed then disappeared back into the alcove.

"Pay her no mind, Talos. Her wounds are not of your making." Wacad touched Talos's weapon sash over his heart. "She chooses to carry the pain of our younger brother's death like a shield against life. She needs more time for them to become mere scars."

"Sure. Never been able to figure out dames." Talos shook his head, but Aidan could feel the sorrow in his raspy voice. "Not about to happen today either."

Aidan needed to know more about Pena. Maybe he could slip away and hunt her down while he explored the finery of the place. Would it be so bad if a bauble or two made its way into his pocket?

"Forget it, runt." A forceful tug pulled him out of the alcove. "No side angles. You're about to meet the magistrate, savvy? Make a good impression for once."

"Savvy, luv. Just checking for escape routes in case his honor unjustly—"

"Forget about it, runt." Talos snapped the pirate by his shirt and pushed him forward into a large, sparsely decorated dining room.

The table was set with oddly shaped dishes and gleaming silverware that caught Aidan's practiced eye. They might not be silver but the unmistakable gleam of precious metals was there. His fingers grew restless but a firm grip on the back of his trousers kept him from exploring their weight just yet.

Three Oracans stood at the far end of the room. All moved to greet them as the brothers entered. Aidan recognized Chakki from earlier. She looked smug and cunning for some reason. He suspected this was her usual expression since it sat on her face so easily.

Another, Tobi, was clearly a hunter like Talos. His lack of clothing and heavy weapons sash covering his bulky chest displayed only a few small weapons. But his right arm, where hunters displayed their tattoos that marked each successful hunt, was adorned almost to the creature's wrist. Aidan needed to ask Talos where the ink was drawn when an arm was full. Tobi greeted Talos like an old friend. Aidan didn't think Talos had any of those outside of the Commander. That made Tobi interesting.

The center of everyone's respectful attention broke away and strode toward them at a swift pace Aidan had not expected from someone old enough to have fathered the four brothers surrounding him to be so active. Menalon was as tall as Talos, his chest larger, his shoulders broader. He was massive as a bull and twice as large again. His robe was worn as a mere cloak, a wisp of fabric anchored in place by raised six-inch talons on his shoulders. The cloth fluttered like wings when he walked. Aidan had the image of a winged dragon descending on him flash through his mind. He fidgeted in place, suddenly anxious and uncertain about his ability to impress or win over any of these monstrous Ceme-like creatures.

"Honor and compassion, my sons." Menalon's voice rumbled like thunder, low, dangerous and hypnotic. Aidan almost joined in the greeting, the voice was so compelling. A violet gaze raked over him, then met his fascinated stare and held it. Nostrils flared, even Menalon's tongue tasted the air around Aidan, violet eyes never blinking. After what felt like a lifetime, Aidan's dry eyes blinked and the rumbling voice broke the silence. "I am Menalon, Patriarch of the Cashe of Menalon."

Aidan just gaped for a moment then stumbled to life. "A bloody dragon, you are, guv! Never saw a real one ta'fore. Tals's more like me Ceme sea god, but you!" His eyes went wide at a new thought.

"Have you got a tail?" He made to peek around the towering creature but a swift swat to his hindquarters and a low throaty growl snapped him back to the gravity of the introduction. "Ah, aye, Captain Aidan Maymon." He flashed a small grin and added, "Pirate." That summed him up in one word. After a pinch to his ass cheek he blurted, "Tis an honor ta meet ya, governor."

Menalon studied the pirate a moment more then turned his gaze to his son. "You have chosen with an eye for chaos. Life will be... unpredictable." The corners of his mouth moved up and his gaze softened. "That is fitting for a revered Hunter of Oracan." He clapped his hands and announced, "The ritual meal will begin."

§ § § §

Once Menalon's blessing was granted, the meal officially signaled the start of the bonding ritual. Talos had explained most of the ceremony and challenges during the trip to the planet, but he was sure Aidan had only been partially listening. Now, he wasn't so sure.

"Are you aware of what our bonding ritual requires of you, pirate?" The harsh tone and disapproving snarl came from Dagi, Menalon's security warrior. Zeban had told Talos there was no support from this quarter. The warrior felt this bonding threatened the purity of the Oracan race. He was deeply aligned with the political sector of Council that had lobbied against Aidan being here. They cared nothing for his life.

Aidan gave the menacing warrior a calm, deliberate glance then made a show of tearing meat from a bone and swallowing before answering, "Aye, do at that, me bucko." Aidan threw the bone on his plate and licked the juices from his fingers. "Weddin' of sorts." He smiled, but Talos saw no warmth in it. He braced himself. It wasn't going to be pretty.

"'Cept, the way ay hear it, the weddin' guests get ta hunt me down and try ta kill me. An' if'n me lonely self escapes with me miserable life intact, ye lot brand me poor body with fire and blood, ink me flesh with magical signs that mark me as property of your band of murderous cutthroats." He dropped his arms to the table and his bounty wrist band caught his eye. "This lovely trinket," he twisted and yanked at it, "is me promise ring, I'm thinkin'. A bit plain for me taste, like things a tad more ornate meself, a little spark and shine, but then *no one asked me* afore it was put on." The pirate grabbed his cup and downed the entire contents of the strong drink. He smacked his lips and looked around the table at the stoic, silent faces, stopping on Talos. "Least me reward 'tis worth runnin' the bloody gauntlet."

"I believe I like your chosen one, Talos. He has a warrior's spirit and speaks plainly. He carries my blessings and support for a victorious challenge." Menalon laughed and most joined him. Dagi did not.

Talos merely bowed his head in acceptance of the great honor. Having Menalon's support was something he hadn't expected. Leave it to his unconventional pirate to win over the usually highly disciplined and unyielding patriarch.

"Still not thrilled about the branding, mind you. No pirate would be, guv." Aidan sounded glum but resigned.

Pena appeared to refill Aidan's cup with the last of a bottle of Earth wine Menalon had obtained for the meal. She was gone before Aidan picked up the cup again. The pirate swirled the red potion around then set it on the table. "Love to, but have ta keep me wits. Got beasties on me scent tonight." He offered the cup to Talos who shook his head.

Menalon took it from Aidan's reluctant fingers and hoisted it in a toast. "A pledge of strength to the bonding." He took one gulp of the sweet liquid, and tossed the cup into the open firepit flickering in the center of the table.

"I recall the pledge made at *our* bonding ritual, Talos." Chakki's face was less chiseled by weather and gender. She looked more like a Tiberian snake at this moment. "I take great pride in that memory."

Their failed bonding was not a topic he had discussed with… anyone. Not his pirate, not even Marius. But he would be now. Chakki was making sure of that.

Surprisingly, Aidan just sprawled in his chair and silently looked between Talos and Chakki as if waiting for a show to begin. Talos's brothers remained passive, clearly used to Chakki's tactics. She had not changed since their forced attempt at mating.

"There was no bond between us. No snare to compel the joining of our blood." Oracans usually didn't feel the snare bind them until the ritual. Fever was lust, plain and simple. The genetic snare was biological imperative. What he had with Aidan was unique and inexplicable. The snare activating before the blood mix. As much as Talos made light of it, he knew they were a special bond pairing unlike all others.

Talos took his gaze off Aidan long enough to throw a half-lidded, daggered glance at Chakki. "And you failed your challenge."

"Not all arranged pairings are successful." She shifted in her seat, slowly smoothing out her robes. "When your pirate fails, maybe the blood bond will be granted to a new chosen one. One who has waited for you. One worthy of the cashe of Menalon. One who would not fail a second time."

"Wouldn' count on it, m'lady." Aidan leered at her, confidence and bravado mixed with a large dose of lust leaked from his pores so strongly Talos almost gasped. Someone else at the table uttered a growl that was instantly choked off.

"Pledged me life to this great sea beast, gave 'em me body, ta be sure." Aidan swung his leg down from the arm of the chair where he had propped it in his casual sprawl. His tone went from light-hearted to deadly serious. "Others have had it 'afore. Just like Tals had you." The smug smile vanished from Chakki's face.

He leaned forward, looking from guest to guest, ignoring the discomfort and poorly hidden mirth displayed. He focused on Chakki. "Gave me soul, this time. Been mine for m'self alone all these years. None have 'ad their hands on it 'til he come along. None other 'twas worth a pirate's pledge. I'll not be failing your heathen challenge, as the horizon stays in the distance. A pirate never gives up his treasure."

Chapter Nine

The rock formations glistened in shades of gray to black like ashes from a spent bonfire. The surface was grainy, the texture of frail, moth-eaten wool. Like the surrounding air, the rocks were overly warm to his touch, almost too warm for bare skin, the heat making itself known through the thick soles of his recently acquired boots.

Aidan shifted his weight, testing the solidarity of the surface. He found it hard as the metal hull of Pathos Six, but with none of the vibrations he could normally detect on the space station. Here the hard, black ground seemed still as the dead.

Glancing at the throng of towering beasts, all silent and gray as tombstones awaiting him a few meters away, Aidan let his mouth quirk into a cocky smile. Walking among the dead only seemed appropriate for a man who should have died centuries ago.

He slowly advanced toward the semi-circle of waiting, unworldly creatures. Needing an anchor in this foreign world, he murmured out loud, letting the sound of his own voice calm him. "Right dreadful welcome party this is."

His gaze flickered over the tallest males, identifying Talos's brothers, Arco, Wacad and Zeban, and his lover's old friend Tobi. Aidan paused when his gaze struck the fierce, disapproving stare of the quiet beast named Dagi. Unease skittered down his spine and he had to work to keep his self-confident smirk in place. Unlike Tobi's open disapproval, Dagi had done little threatening toward Aidan, but Aidan noticed the way the Oracan's gaze weighed heavily on him whenever they were in each other's presence. He couldn't decide if it was distrust or curiosity in the beast's violet stare.

Just then light winds picked up, bringing with them a faint hissing sound. Another ripple of unease crawled over his flesh. Aidan shrugged to loosen the hold of Dagi's glare. He could still recognize a soul with murderous intent.

No longer interested in the faces of the remaining Oracans, Aidan dropped his own gaze, focusing on the uneven rock beneath his boots as he moved into the circle of gray.

As he walked, he tried to find a rhythm in the hissing wind, but gusts of hot air buffeted the rocks in irregular waves, slicing tiny threads off as it cut through the millions of porous stone. A choir of mystical sea sirens popped into his head, forcing a shudder to run across his shoulders. Nothing was more unnerving to a seafaring man than the specter of dreaded sirens calling a sailor to an early grave. He shook his head to clear away the vision, to focus on other, more pleasant things.

Behind him, the black Oracan sea, fueled by an underground hot bed, shimmered in the starlight, the sound of the waves measured and soothing, the one reminder of Aidan's faraway past life. The smell of the water wasn't the salt air of Earth, but Aidan imagined it still carried the tang of freedom and adventure in it.

The wind slipped over his skin, its warmth caressing his naked chest and bare arms. It plucked at the thin fabric of his trousers, incessant like the unwelcome hands of a drunken trollop. The wind shifted again, howling now, sending strands of his chin length hair to hide his face. He darted a glance through the sudden curtain of hair, searching for the one piercing scowl he actually wanted to see. No, *needed* to see.

"Where be you, you bloody, hulking, sea beastie?"

And just like that, Talos was there, waiting, standing on a raised slab of black rock in the center of his brethren near a bowl on a stone pedestal. Tall torches stuttered and smoked, their spear-like handles thrust into natural openings in the rock surrounding the proud hunter.

Tall, broad, his chest rippling with each deep breath he took, Talos looked like a living statue carved from dense wood weathered a pale gray.

The nubs of cartilage on his oiled chest and scalp caught the glow from a dozen or more torches lighting the night. The smooth, oval patches shone, iridescent as the finest pearls the oceans had to offer. It had taken Aidan weeks to realize the hard, smooth patches of cartilage, like sun-warmed stones under Aidan's rope-callused hands, hid one of the most sensitive areas on his lover's thick-skinned body. With proper attention, they turned the stoic warrior into a passionate, caring beast in their bedchamber.

Aidan longed to touch the massive creature. He wanted to hear Talos growl with pleasure. The mere sight of Talos made him hard with need, despite the audience. His cock hardened, lengthening within the confines of his trousers, heedless of the prying eyes on him.

Small gusts of wind carried a variety of smells, most of which Aidan couldn't identify, but mixed in with the tang of sweat, sea and sand was an odor he was becoming very good at recognizing. His body responded to it even before his brain identified it—the scent of his lover's arousal. He'd been able to smell his lover's presence before actually seeing Talos for several weeks. It was both disturbing and thrilling.

Right now, Aidan decided to concentrate on the thrilling part.

Strolling toward the group, gaze fixed on Talos's features, Aidan skirted several hunters who had moved to the outer edge of the arena. A quick glance at the crowd told him more than one male here had a gleam of hate in their gazes. That he had expected. It was the one or two lustful glares that surprised him, adding to his growing unease.

He understood the distrust and loathing, the need some of the Oracans had to expel him from their world. But he didn't understand any of them wanting to claim him for themselves. He was a ship's captain and a freeman. Regardless of the band on his wrist, he wasn't a prize to be won or a lowly cabin boy to be used. He and he alone picked his bedmates. Or mate. One mate. Single mate. Talos. Only Talos.

After boldly adjusting the thickening cock in his pants, Aidan stalked toward the center of the arena where he had been told to present himself. No one challenged him as he made his way to Talos's side, though Jak stepped into his path. Aidan threw Jak a hard stare as he deftly navigated around him without breaking his stride.

Climbing the four steep stone slabs up to the top, Aidan gave Talos a saucy grin.

"'Bout time they let me see you. Was beginning to think you'd run out on me, luv."

Remembering the strict rules of the trial ritual Oracan culture demanded he follow, Aidan stepped in close to his lover. The ritual demanded the mating pair keep their hands to themselves during the initial ceremony, so instead Aidan let his bare chest press against Talos's hard abdomen, enjoying the slickness of their sweaty flesh sliding together. He ignored the dark growls of disapproval behind him.

The scent of sex and excitement hung so thickly in the hot, humid air even Aidan could smell it. He let a needy groan escape, thrilled by the way Talos pressed closer in response. The hunter inhaled deeply, leaning down so he hovered over Aidan's upturned face, lips tantalizingly close.

"You should worry more about my catching you, Runt."

"Lookin' forward to it."

A low, throbbing drum beat started, accompanied by a sudden, eerie chanting of the deep, penetrating voices of the males surrounding them. The primitive song combined with the hissing wind, and the flickering firelight, Aidan felt almost at home here. The rawness of the planet and the warrior code of honor of the Oracan matched his own skewed, but vaguely honorable, view of life. In many ways accepting Talos's people as his own was the most natural thing that had occurred since his abduction from Earth.

Acting as preceptor for the ritual, Zeban stepped up beside

the pair. Neither Aidan nor Talos broke away to acknowledge his presence. Amused, he noisily cleared his throat. "The time to begin the ritual has arrive. Let honor and duty forge your new path."

The drum beat stilled as the chanting abruptly halted, magnifying the hissing winds. Aidan tried to suppress the shudder that jarred his shoulders, but failed. A branding iron rested in the firepit beside them. His gaze darted to Talos's to see his reaction. Expecting Talos to be alarmed at his unease, Aidan was surprised, and slightly hurt, when the hunter's expression didn't change.

Talos leaned closer, his mouth parted and lips moist enough to glisten in the light. "I could smell your fear from the moment we arrived on the planet, Aidan. You've held yourself well despite it, runt. The best warriors know fear can be a powerful aid for survival. Use it to your advantage. There are things here that *should* be feared."

Aidan relaxed. Casting a quick mischievous glance at a waiting Zeban, he extended his arms out to his sides to prove he wasn't using his hands and bounced up on the balls of his feet to plant a quick lick across Talos' sensitive chest plates. "Case ya forget 'bout why I'm riskin' life an' limb."

§ § § §

"As Talos of Menalon's declared mate in the sacred Ritual of Toget, The Joining, Aidan of Maymon, come forward. You must present your sacrifice to the bond." Zeban indicated a stone near the fire pit for Aidan to sit on.

The pirate moved from Talos's side, dark eyes drawn to the red-hot iron in the fire. The branding was primal, savage and very Oracan. Aidan accepted it, but he still feared the touch of the metal to his skin. He'd seen a branding or two in his time. The smell of seared flesh and the cries of the men had never left him. He hoped he could keep silent. This audience wouldn't be keen on weakness of any kind.

Taking his seat on the stone, Aidan jumped slightly as a coolness stuck his bare left shoulder. Wacad was there, rubbing an ointment into his skin. It tingled, then burned for a brief moment. He gave the healer a nervous, crooked smile and said, "Best leave some for after, Doc. Don't know 'bout beasties, but iron leaves a powerful wound on a man."

"You will endure."

Aidan snickered. Best to keep it jolly while he could. "True 'nough. Can't say as a body will like it though."

"You claim a place in the Cashe of Menalon. You have the right to take strength from our growing snare." Talos was there, kneeing before him.

A startled murmur rippled through the witnesses and guests. Existence of the snare within two Oracan's before they mixed blood was very rare. Between an Oracan and another species was not to be imagined.

Zeban cut it off, proclaiming, "Existence of the snare within Talos *and* his chosen one, *a non-Oracan*, prior to the ritual is rare before they have given sacrifice in the blood ceremony." Aidan saw the surprise flicker across Zeban's face, but he recovered quickly, like a true diplomat. "Because of this special genetic gift, Talos of Menalon has the right to share the honor of his mate's cashe mark."

The hunter took Aidan's forearms in his own massive grip and held them to the stone pedestal between them. Talos grabbed the bounty band and Aidan's wrist, twining his fingers around the metal. He dropped his voice so low Aidan had to strain to hear it. "Hold on tight and concentrate on nothing but me. Savvy?"

"Savvy, you great, bloody beast."

Wacad touched Aidan's shoulder with a warm, light poke. "It begins, little pirate. Sit very still."

"All present here tonight bear witness to the mark of Menalon bestowed upon the chosen mate of Talos, fourth son of Menalon, revered Hunter, child of Oracan."

Aidan heard the sizzle of metal being tested for temperature. A shudder ran down his spine. His wrist was clamped in a vise. His closed his eyes and focused on his lover's scent, the warmth radiating off his hulking mass, the weight of his hands in a death grip with his own. Anything to block out the swish of robes behind him. He didn't want to think about what was coming, how his flesh would curl and char, too damaged to even blister. How—?

Stop!

The command rang in his head, interrupting the growing urge to run from this barbaric cruelty. Ink was fine, he'd had a few of his own before the domineering Dr. Jaclyn had somehow removed them. They were symbolic. A rite of passage for a young man, pirate or not. But branding. Branding was to be feared and avoided.

Stop!

There it was again. Aidan's eyelids flew open wide, his eyes darting back and forth at the surrounding darkness looking for the source of the voice. When it came again he realized it was in his head and no one but he could hear it.

Runt!

Aidan locked stares with his lover. Talos pulled at the band on Aidan's wrist, gripping it so tightly Aidan knew they would both bear the bruises for it later.

Focus.

Stunned by this new witchcraft, Aidan hesitated only a moment. *Knew you 'twere a Ceme god! Knew it!*

He stared into Talos's eyes, startled to see the inner lids fall down, making the hunter's eyes yellow. Aidan felt a rush of calm flow over him, a blanket of warmth surrounding him. Pressure dug into his left shoulder just where his arm joined his body. The air filled with the provocative odor of his lover's body, pushing away everything but the presence of his glorious, bewitching hunter-sea-god. Aidan floated secure and calm, only marginally aware when it recessed. Reality came back with a rush of sound and a deep burning in his shoulder. The branding was done.

Peering cautiously over his shoulder, Aidan was pleased to see the swirls and ridges just like part of Talos's larger tattoo, burned into his skin. The area was a fiery red and the burning went deep but not intolerable. The night was full of surprises and it was just getting started.

"You did well, little pirate," Wacad whispered in his ear as he soothed the fresh wound with more salve. "Amazingly so."

Holding the smoking iron high for all to see, Zeban declared, "The family crest of Menalon forever marks this chosen one as a member of our cashe, no matter the outcome of the challenges yet to be met. Honor and compassion, Aidan of Menalon!"

Aidan stumbled to his feet and awkwardly returned the greeting he had seen Talos do so many times. His armed ached with each movement, but pride overrode pain at the joyous frown on his dour hunter's face.

Zeban took center stage again. "The Ritual of Toget begins. All challengers declare yourselves."

The night was cooler than the day time. The sea breeze added a momentary gust of moisture to the air. A light sweat sheen made Aidan's skin glow in the firelight as he flexed his wiry muscles and stretched his lean frame.

Still feeling the effects of Talos's earlier magic spell, Aidan felt a strength within him. He concentrated on it, urged it to grow. If magic was a part of it, he was grateful for it, no matter how much it unnerved him. He would need every advantage the gods could grant him to defeat these murderous beasties.

All four of them.

"Declare." Zeban gestured to the first one who had stepped eagerly forward.

"Dagi of Meollege. Security Council. I challenge for the Sector of Pell, in the united effort to keep the purity of the Oracan bloodlines."

"Dagi, are you not to be with Menalon?" Zeban demanded.

"Menalon fell ill after the meal." Wacad stepped forward, concern in his puzzled glance. "He requests the presence of his healer when his duties to the ritual have ended. A double guard has been assigned to him in my absence with Menalon's permission."

Arco quietly left the ritual arena after a whispered conversation with Wacad.

Zeban watched but said nothing until Wacad nodded to him. "Challenger accepted. Declare."

Stol stepped out of the shadows. "Stol of Jannna, Council of Trade. I challenge to reclaim the honor of Chakki of Por."

That caused a wave of murmurs and growls. Trying to unseat a chosen one was common, but rarely was it done by a surrogate. Oracan were expected to fight their own battles.

Stol hastened to add, "She has the right of prior claim. I will restore her family honor."

"Not bloody likely, mate," Aidan called out. "But if by some turn of fate, ye do win, *honor* is all she'll get. Tals has no taste for mean-spirited harlots."

Zeban held up a hand to quiet the exchange. He solemnly announced, "Challenger accepted. Declare." A third call went out and was answered.

"Jak of Stonf, Warrior, Security Council. I challenge to claim the chosen one as my own." The warrior was muscle bound and trained, but he was a soldier. A dull mind and lack of imagination marked a military man in the pirate's day. He doubted that had changed much.

Talos growled, a low, menacing, thunderous sound that made Aidan's spine tingle and his cock leap. It was nearly impossible not to tackle his possessive lover to the ground there and then.

Zeban cut short the declarations with a curt, "Challenger accepted."

That left one.

"Declare."

"Tobi of Tiia, Hunter, Council of Details. I lay challenge to this mating because I must."

"Challenger accepted. Declare."

Silence finally fell.

Aidan sighed in relief. Four was more than enough. He had

expected Dagi. Stol was a surprise. He had struck Aidan as too jittery to fight well. It was good to have an easy opponent in the horde if he had to fight them all. Jak wasn't a total surprise. He'd seen the lust in that one's eyes. He made Aidan cautious. A man with cardinal wants could be more dangerous than one with mere needs. Tobi, Talos's childhood friend, was the most unlikely challenger. He had seen the light of unexpected betrayal in his mate's narrowed stare. He sympathized. He'd been there, too. Perkin's ugly, mutinous, turncoat face danced in his thoughts until Zeban's commanding, cultured voice snapped him back to his current reality.

He was ready to fight for his lover. And his life.

Chapter Ten

The challenge was to simply be the first to reach the top of a cliff by a gorge where the next part of the challenge awaited. Once there, spiritual demons would be confronted and their power cast off to prevent them from impacting the coming bond. It was all witchcraft and sorcery to Aidan. He had no demons he was willing to part with.

It sounded simple. Make it through a cave, up a cliff, and then over a gorge to reach the platform at the top where a new challenge would be presented. He needed to find the right cave that led to the right cliff that gave him a gorge with plateau. The instructions were straight forward if sparse on detail. Stamina and speed were familiar allies, but now, while this strange fever dogged him, it was more problematic.

Problems were the theme of the evening. Aidan had been unprepared for the transporter beam that had whisked him from the dry, hot planet's surface to drop him at a far-off place. Eyes tightly closed, he'd endured the process in darkness. He knew he had traveled far because he could no longer smell his hunter or sense his warm and domineering bulk nearby. A pit of emptiness filled his gut. He felt alone for the first time in a long while. Alone save for four opponents licking at his boots.

At the tap of Zeban's ceremonial bong, the challenge began.

The surface of this new wilderness was different than the ritual arena. The ground under his boots was steeper, the sand rockier, and the night sky clearer, more heavily dotted with stars. Stars were a seafaring man's best friends. He had studied Oracan constellations before coming. It was good to have friends waiting.

"Where be ya, me pretty?" Talking to himself was a lifetime habit he saw no reason to break. "Give this lonesome pirate an anchor for his journey." He searched for a pinpoint of stability to guide his progress. He crowed out loud when one overly bright light revealed itself in the forest of glittering lights. "There be you. Call you, Men'lon, father of all dragons." He chuckled at his own joke, then sobered and hoped the ailing older Oracan was well. He was a frightful beastie. But a frightful beastie in the family could be useful. He mentally marked his location against the stars and ignored everyone else around him.

Aidan took the high ground leaving his heftier challengers behind. The Oracan's had the upper hand of being conditioned to the dry air and terrain, but he had been shipwrecked and marooned before this. High ground at night was of limited use, but a gorge was created by running water and that could be smelt and heard, and high ground would help find those clues.

The slight breeze was pleasantly warm. It carried with it the scampering of many legs creatures and the call of more than one night predator. Aidan kept a hand on his blade hilt and his ear to the occasional skittering of loose dirt running parallel to his left. It was only a faint evidence of an opponent, skilled and experienced. He tagged Dagi or Tobi for that one. Both were worthy challengers.

Verging off to his right, the smell of Jak's powerful musk retreated along with the faint shushing sound his flapping groin covering made as he ran. Aidan was pleased to rid of that one at the moment.

Stol must be so far behind Aidan couldn't detect him. He was the weakest danger, but a danger nonetheless. Underestimating an enemy could find you going off a cliff instead of over it.

Aidan corrected his course once, moving north as best he could. On a dry planet, water was usually at the colder regions, where moisture gathered. Talos had shown him moving painting of rain so cold it froze. Near the far north. He doubted it snowed here, but north was still his best bet for water. And he was a betting man.

§ § §

The river was narrow and deep, tucked into a gorge covered in foliage and thick vines. Climbing the steep walls had been as easy as navigating a sail's elaborate rigging and tangled nets, though a bit longer than a climb to the *Maid's* nest. Aidan was nearly winded and his arms trembled from excursion. Even the fresh brand on his shoulder throbbed with a dull ache that penetrated to the bone.

Navigating the rugged cliff side in the dark was slow going, but Aidan couldn't detect anyone on his heels yet. Sweat beaded on his forehead, running down his temples to trickle across his now scratched and bleeding bare chest.

It felt good to smell the plants, to feel the rough bark and the silky leaves of living things. He missed being among nature, the touch of a whispery breeze on his skin. Pathos Six was a fine berth, but he missed sunshine, the sea and the rock of his ship beneath him. A bit of dirt under his nails was a reminder of the small joys of his old life.

Two moons had erupted in the night sky once Aidan had cleared the narrow, angled clifftop. Hung low, barely higher than the horizon, they cast an eerie, but welcome glow over the foreign landscape. Shadows lurked at the edges of the barren plateau, the surface barely larger than a ship's cuddy. Only one man at a time could safely lay on this wee island of rock.

A single stone bowl rested on a large flat rock at the center of the clifftop. Parched from fever and the long climb, Aidan smelled it, dipped his fingers into the cool liquid then, satisfied it probably wasn't poison, he drank from it. Oracan demon juice. He hoped it had alcohol in it. The taste of fruit was tart. It made his mouth dry and his tongue feel thick, but it soothed his dry throat. His stomach queased a bit, but no more than any of the Oracan foods had done to him at dinner.

A wave of exhaustion hit him. Flattened him to the ground. Like a sudden undercurrent, Aidan was dragged down as it rolled and boiled. There was no air to be had, his limbs weighed down, his body crushed under a hard, unyielding burden he couldn't push away. He could see the clear night sky, but the stars that had been kind to him earlier blinked and shimmered into familiar faces of the long dead.

They came to life before him, memories of his past Earthly life rushing by in a jumble of color, pain and emotion. Scenes of his harsh and lonely childhood, his mother's early death, and his first taste of the lash at the hands of a heartless captain.

Life sped in fast forward until he was, again, fighting for his life against his mutinous crew. The grizzled, scarred face of Nate Sterns, his trusted first mate, stared up at him from the ship's deck, lifeless and bloodied, the last to fall under the accursed Perkins's mutinous sword. Anger and loss filled Aidan's chest, tightening the stranglehold on his mind and body.

Suddenly, hands were on him, groping him, yanking at his trousers, griping his hair hard enough to force his head back to allow demanding lips to taste his flesh. Aidan searched his memories for this stifling assault from his past, but could not latch on to any event that matched it. He supposed it must be what would have happened if Perkins had had his way with him. How he hated that backstabbing, son of a jackass, ugly bastard!

He felt himself bodily raised up and the vision of struggling against being thrown overboard raced into his mind. Fighting back, Aidan kicked and squirmed, fist and boot finally connecting with a solid body. Marginally free of the weight pressing him to the ground, he found the hilt of the blade at his waist. He'd longed to give Perkins his due. Even in a hallucination, it would be a satisfying end to the heinous cutthroat.

Seemingly engulfed by Perkins's brawny arms and foul smell, Aidan lashed out with his blade, content to inflict any damage he could on the other pirate. A surprised humph blew into his ear, the odor a musky stench. Then a sharply angled face, blurry and dark, invaded his vision. Blurry, but not so much so that Aidan couldn't tell it wasn't Perkins. Or any other human. It was Jak, the lustful one.

The massive chest rolled off him with a thud leaving behind a slick, warm wetness on the pirate's skin. The rasp of labored breathing to his right grated on his ear, loud and unnatural.

Aidan fought the now fading mist of hallucination, shaking his head to clear it, gasping in lungfuls of damp night air to gather his senses together again. Strong incessant fingers clawed at his arm, his brand screaming in agony as sharp nails dug into the raw flesh. He twisted and curled, launching his boot heels at the mass that threatened to overtake him again. Jak released him and Aidan rolled away, kicking at anything he could, slicing at shadows, blade gleaming in the white rays of spotty moonlight. He found the edge of the clifftop and he stilled his scrambling crawl.

To his left came the sound of rock and sand crumbing down to the river gorge below, then the crack of branches snapping and a faint splash of water below. The air was still, the only loud breathing came from his own heaving chest. He was flushed with heat, his wounds were on fire, his skin raw in patches over his entire upper torso, his mouth so dry he couldn't find the moisture to spit with.

"So this 'tis what it feels like to be a seven hundred year old pirate." Clutching his blade, Aidan dragged himself from the cliff edge, back to the center of the tiny air island and lay down. No energy could be wasted on what had just happened. It was done and over with. A life lost in battle. A fitting death for any warrior. A groan escaped his cut lips. "Shoulda drunk more rum when ay had a chance."

Staring up into the starlight sky, he found his anchor twinkling brightly. "Men'lon, father of all dragons, I need me monstrous beastie." He glanced into the darkness near the cliff edge then sighed, "Hell of a weddin' day." His eyes drooped shut.

In his dreams, his own ugly, wonderful, Ceme God came and scooped him up to carry him off, growling, "Conniving, little lunatic!" The coolness of thick gray skin was heavenly, even if it wasn't real.

§ § § §

Aidan awoke in an unfamiliar bed, firm matting and silky bedding, the way he liked a berth. If it swayed a bit with the roll of the sea, he'd like it even better. As the evenings events flooded back to him in snips and bits, he realized he was lucky to be breathing, let alone lounging in a grand bed.

Judging by the size of the room and the smell of in the air, he suspected he was in Menalon's home again. The place had a tang of well-oiled weapons and heady spice he'd experienced the first time here but didn't recognize. He now decided to name it 'dragon's bane' because it suited his sense of merriment.

Voices murmured outside the partially open bedroom door. He recognized the low growl of his lover's voice spitting back and forth with two others using rasps and growls that made up the harsh Oracan language. It could have been a fierce argument or an exchange of cooking recipes for all the pirate could understand it.

Either way it reaffirmed what his sense of smell had already told him, his hunter was near. That knowledge soothed the aching pain in his chest. Not the aches caused by the vast array of claw marks, burns and raw abrasions he felt covering his torso, but a dark, heavy thing akin to sorrow. Talos need to know…everything.

Willing himself up and out of bed, the pirate began to leave the room then as an afterthought returned and slipped into his trousers lying on a carved wooden stand. He struggled into his new boots Talos had bought him, briefly wishing for his old, battered ones that required no effort to slog into.

He slipped into the smaller sitting room and all eyes turned to him instantly. Zeban and Arco stood shoulder to shoulder, now struck silent in mid-sentence. Wacad had been walking to the outer door but came back into the room at Aidan's entrance, concern in the kind eyes. Even Pena, Menalon's dagger-eyed servant skulked on the fringes of the room. Aidan didn't care about any of them. Didn't care what they thought, didn't care what they said.

The pirate launched himself off the ground. Talos caught him in midair and pulled him gently to his chest, a soft 'ta-ti' clicked and gurgled into Aidan's shoulder again and again. The pirate closed his eyes and dissolved into the embrace, arms and legs wrapped securely around his lover.

When he did pull back to look Talos in the face, he gave the beast a small, cheerless smile and whispered, "'Twer late to the party, luv. Had to handle it on me own terms, if ya get me drift."

"You met the challenge with honor, runt. A battle hard fought and fairly won."

He was sure there would be a fuss made of Jak's death. Aidan slipped out of the hunter's grasp, reluctant to disengage so quickly, but aware both of them were feeling the sexual pull of the incessant, damnedable snare. They had been separated here longer than at any other point since the beast had kidnapped him. Aidan found himself longing for his lover's tender-rough touch and glorious cock.

"There be no magistrate's purse to fatten over it?"

A small gasp drew all attention to Pena. Uncomfortable under everyone's watchful stare, she came forward and offered Aidan a cup. "More of your Earth drink. I thought it would be welcome after your...challenge."

Hesitant, Aidan slowly accepted the drink. He smelled it, tasted a sip then tossed back the entire contents. Turning to give Pena the cup back, he found she was gone from the room. He shrugged his shoulders, winching at the discomfort in them. He preferred the weak wine to her company anyway. She gave him the chills, like an old voodoo moma he had known in Jamaica.

"We don't pay off tribunals...courts, Aidan." Zeban took the cup from him, his patient tone edged with equal parts amusement and exasperation. "It was clear to all who observed. Jak's death was a result of his own behavior."

"Observed, mate? You can do that? Outside? From far away?" This was something the pirate had never thought of, despite the fact he knew Pathos Six had moving paintings of goin' ons in places all over the station. Aidan felt haunted with the need to make sure Talos really understood. "Was drugged. Hallucinations hit like a storm swell. I-I thought the hunter was Perkins. I was fightin' for me life, luv."

Talos pressed his forehead to Aidan and all the fear drained from the pirate's soul. There would be no questioning of his innocent involvement in Jak's death. No black cloud of mistrust or doubt hanging over his head. He had only a moment to bask in the feeling of relief before civil war broke out among the brothers and his lover stepped away.

"There are always observers to the ritual, Aidan. It must be documented that all who take part do so with honor. The Oracan code must prevail over all." Arco joined the reassurances. He spared his younger brother an admonishing glance. "Talos would have told you of that practice had he been more in touch with his own culture."

"I'm jake on Oracan ritual, brother. I just don't weigh the runt down with things he doesn't have a grip on yet. Like the invention of the camera. He hasn't got the dope on somethings yet. Don't rush him. Seven hundred years is a lot to play catch up on."

"You could show Aidan those things here—" Zeban, ever the diplomat, tried to calm the discussion.

"I spend enough time here."

Zeban wasn't to be distracted. "—And less time out of touch on a remote Corporate station. It was fortunate you were here with Menalon taking ill so suddenly."

"The dragon's ill?" Alarm rushed through Aidan. He liked the imposing patriarch. "Scary, mind you, but a right fine lord, he is. 'Twas in the pink o' health earlier."

Arco nodded at his healer brother. "Wacad has been caring for him. Not everything at the earlier meal agreed with him. Possibly the Earth wine. He will recover."

"Don't change the subject." Talos crossed his beefy arms and glared defiantly. "P6 is perfect. Accepting. No one there cares who I mate." Talos walked over to stand beside Aidan who had perched himself on the arm of a massive throne-like chair, enjoying the lively action. The pirate was quite content to watch the brothers bicker like human families did. Beside him, Wacad silently applied a healing salve to his many cuts and burns, inspecting the pirate intently, making small, unhappy sounds in the back of his throat.

Talos continued his rant unchecked. "Unlike here where pain, suffering and near-death rituals are needed to prove a guy is worthy of being loved. And in case you palookas missed it, Aidan is the one that brought me to Oracan, he's not keeping me away. I had zero intention of ever mating until the snare tied us together."

"You would better understand the Council's thoughts on this bonding if you were near."

"What's to understand? The Council should butt out."

Wacad finally broke his silence. "Seriously, Talos. Aidan is the first *ever* offworlder to bond with an Oracan. The first *human to touch* an Oracan. To be affected by our *genetic snare*. How can you say the Council should ignore this?"

"It's easy. I just say it."

"Excuse me, gents." Aidan swayed to his feet. His bones ached, his wounds ached, and he felt a vague, disturbing need to wash away the grim and smell of Jak's body lingering on him. He half suspected the odor was part of Talos's unreasonable behavior. Any reminder of the other hunter's assault needed to be dealt with sooner than later. He felt a fresh burst of energy. "Need a wash and a piss. Someone be so kind as ta give me a course for the nearest a rain closet."

Chapter Eleven

Aidan was hot, bruised, and sweaty. Having spent the last twelve hours running from various pursuers, evading capture and demonstrating his ability to out think the Oracan brutes on his hindquarters, had left him flying on the energy that came with a satisfying battle. He truly missed a rousing good bar-fight or a few slashes with a fine sword.

At least here he could carry a weapon and not be chastised or frowned at. He could even spit when he liked! No prissy Dr. Jaclyn to tatter on about *progress* and *civility*. It was good to be back among men— well males— that saw things the way they really were and valued a good healthy brawl now and then. Even if several of them wanted to kill him. Not like he hadn't been there before. Made him feel right at home.

Battle scared and pleased with himself, Aidan really wanted a strong cup of grog and some uninterrupted time with Talos. A naked, eager Talos. But his lusty hunter was attending to more official appointed duties. Aidan doubted he'd see Talos any time soon. The Oracan did like their rituals and talk! They were almost as bad as the British when it came to pompous displays of power and strength. Oracans just wore a lot less clothes doing it.

Personally, Aidan preferred cunning and guile. Both qualities had served him well these last twenty-some years. Though brute strength *would* have come in handy dealing with his mutinous crew. He'd liked to have wrung Perkins' neck when the man had leered in his face and thrown him overboard to the sharks. Even now, hundreds of years later, Aidan wished he could go back in time and give that murderous bastard his just end. Maybe, one day he'd find a way. After all, few were better at being devious than pirate Captain Aidan Maymon!

That was probably why Talos had insisted Aidan come back to their quarters instead of waiting for him. Talos didn't want him getting restless. Aidan was too good at finding things to occupy his time when he was restless. The hulking bugger was probably afraid of any more *unfortunate mishaps*, as brother Zeban had diplomatically put it earlier, happening again.

Suddenly miffed, Aidan began stripping off his filthy clothes, throwing them to the far corners of the room. Never one for internal dialogue when his voiced worked just fine, with or without an audience, he let his thoughts slip out uncensored.

"How could an entire bloody race of creatures be born with no sense of merriment in their thick hides? Buggers need to lower their high 'n mightiness. Where is the jolly in that? Needs someone to teach them 'bout the pleasures they be missing out on!"

Down to mud-streaked flesh, he twisted the only thing left on his body, the metal band around his wrist that showed he was the bounty of an Oracan Hunter.

He grinned. "Tals said I should do something constructive with my free time here." His grin spread wider. "Looks like it be up to me to teach them." He laughed, a satisfied sway to his walk as he headed for the adjoining, smaller room off the bedroom. His fingers never left the hated bracelet.

The first few weeks after Talos had captured him, he had worn an angry red abrasion on his skin from trying to work the metal off. The only thing that had kept him from cutting off his own hand to remove it was the fact that Talos had saved his life when the hunter stole him from a watery, painful death by shark and drowning. His honor demanded he give his life over to his savior and Talos demanded Aidan wear the band. But Aidan didn't have to be happy about it!

The band marked him as a hunter's prize, removable only by an Oracan. Talos insisted it protected him from others, but in Aidan's mind it was just another form of the brand pirate hunters had marked their captors with during his time on Earth. This was just less painful and disfiguring than a P burned into his forehead. Though it was just as damning. It meant he wasn't a free man any longer.

Not one to waste time on unpleasant things, Aidan turned his thoughts and his hands to more enjoyable pursuits. He ran his fingers though the grime and sweat on his flushed skin. He was spoiled now, like a dainty governor's daughter. He actually longed for the opportunity to use the magic rain closet. He'd always liked the feel of rain on his skin and this was the only place he had found it in this glass and metal world. Plus the pounding water and closed doors to the closet provided him the opportunity to pleasure himself unseen and unheard.

The usual increase in his desire for sex over the last few months kept him in a nearly constant state of arousal. The need for release had begun to outweigh the need for sleep or food. And the problem with self-gratification was that the release of tension and need never lasted very long. Aidan found himself distractingly hard and wanting only hours later. Only after an intense and lengthy coupling with his stoic lover did the now painful urge to mate fade away for any measurable period of time. As much as Aidan enjoyed coupling, it was exhausting.

Even now his cock was achingly hard, leaking pearls of creamy white. He yearned for the delicious brandy taste of Talos's lips and tongue, the feel of the hunter's strong hands on his hips, holding him down, forcing him to be still long enough to be pleasured properly. Holding him steady so that amazing serpent of a cock could snake its way into his body, doing things to him no human man had ever done. Sex, coupling, making love had never been like it was with Talos. Just the idea of having the heady scent of Oracan sweat and the bittersweet taste of the warrior's loins on his tongue made Aidan's mouth water and his cock throb with need.

Aidan stumbled to the rain closet. A shower of warm droplets immediately began falling from the tiny holes in the roof of the large stone lined room. He grinned.

Ducking under the spray, he wasted no time on needless foreplay.

Stroking his stiff cock in a harsh, rapid pace, he paid no mind to the grime on his scratched, bruised palms until the sensitive flesh rebelled at the abuse. Pain pushed the heat of insistent pleasure away so it remained nothing but a mild ember at the base of his swollen cock.

Frustrated, Aidan gave in to his body's annoying demands to provide more than hurried stimulation. Dipping his fingers into the soft, pasty soap contained in a shallow indentation in the wall, he slathered his torso with the slop until a silky foam covered his hairless chest.

The soap's spicy scent released by the water teased his nostrils. He inhaled deeply. Some of the tension slipped away. He slowed from a harsh scrubbing of his lower abdomen to a sensual exploration of his rib-cage and then moved on to his already taut and aching nipples. The sexual heat reignited deep in his gut with every twist and plucking caress of his callused fingertips.

This felt so good. He twisted the nubs harder, relishing the hot flush of burning pain. His cock throbbed so tightly he was aware of his pulse beating at the base. Aidan moaned, the desperate sound loud in his head, but muffled by the stone walls and rushing water.

Licking his dry lips, he closed his eyes and imagined the hands on him belonging to Talos. Large, powerful, meaty hands that caressed and teased his body better than any tavern keeper whore ever had. Hands that could crush his bones, carry his full weight without pause. Hands that had taught him the profit in lingering on the way to gaining gratification and release. Hands he wished were on him now.

Sliding through the silky foam, he worked the suds over his smooth, hard belly, then down to his groin. Drawing circles in the green froth, he teased the base of his cock, washing away dirt and sweat. Each pass of his hand released the cool spicy scent of the soap. It made his skin tighten, bringing a tingle to it.

Enjoying the feel of it, he cupped his sac, squirming at the delightful rush of sensation as his balls swelled and his sac contracted around them, pulling up, flushed with heat. Eyes flashing open,

Aidan stumbled back until his shoulders hit a wall. Bracing himself against the stone wall, he basked in the warmth of the vigorous waterfall. His cock ached, the head swollen, deep red next to the brown of his shaft, the beads of white seed washing away as fast as they pooled in the tiny porthole.

One hand abandoned his nipples to grasp his shaft, gathering a generous coating of the pasty soap first. He gasped at the first touch, groaning and hissing as his already tight flesh reacted with the foam. Climax burned deep in his gut, a dull fiery buzz that made him squirm. But the buzz stayed low, insistent, heady, making him dizzy and weak, restless and distracted with a need mere cock play wouldn't appease. His body was never happy with solo efforts anymore. His ass clenched, the muscles spasming, his body begging to be filled, taken.

Rolling his branded shoulder over the water drenched walls, Aidan faced the stone wall, raw chest plastered to the warm rock, temple and bruised cheek pressed to the surface for stability. One soap-filled hand grasped his shaft while the other slipped from his sac to the fluttering opening between his ass cheeks. Foam slicked fingers circled the opening, teasing his eager flesh the way Talos had taught him to enjoy a bit of play before the deed.

The fiery tingle from the soap exploded along the sudsy trail from his balls to puckered hole causing the buzz of brewing climax to boil deeper in his gut. He thrust two fingers into the willing rosebud of muscle and nerves, hissing at the sudden stab of pain/pleasure. Moving his finger in short jabs, he threw away any more thought of lingering play to search for the spot that Talos always managed to find straight off. The place that was guaranteed to send him off like a cannon shot. He worked hard, thrusting and twisting, but the pleasure spot eluded him. His need for release grew stronger, but the buzz within his gut refused to do more than snap and sizzle like water splashed on a blacksmith's hot forge. Skin flushed, his breath came in shallow, desperate pants, white spots dancing under his clenched eyelids.

"Bloody hell!" He stroked deeper, the angle hard to maintain standing up. Pumping his cock faster, he rolled his face over the stone, pulling up the vision of his huge, beastly lover, imagining it was Talos's hard body pressing him to the wall, the hunter's skilled tongue on his neck, and the Oracan's amazing snakelike cock entering his body, sliding along his insides, turning his guts and free will to sawdust. But even the most vivid imagining wasn't close enough to the real thing to grant Aidan release.

"For the love of bastard sea serpents with their horny toad cocks an' grabby tentacles!" His waiting orgasm simmered and rolled in his groin, sending out flashes of pleasure so bright and sharp his knees weakened. He pressed more heavily against the wall and moaned, "Where the bloody hell are you, you great gray bastard?"

He sagged against the wall. He had to quickly withdraw his fingers to catch himself before he slid to the floor of the stall. He groaned, a low, pitiful sound of defeat.

"A man should be able to pleasure himself *by* himself now an' then!" He slowed the hand on his shaft, then released it with one frustrated swirl and pinch of the weeping tip. He slapped the wall supporting him with an open palm, swearing a string of foul oaths only a pirate could create, ending with a venomous, "Ruddy, overgrown monster has ruined me for life!"

He pushed off the wall, preparing to finish his washing and leave. As his hands left the wall his back slammed into another hard surface. Strong arms wrapped around his waist, rock hard muscle and bone molding to his slight frame, enfolding him in a blanket of hot, slick Oracan flesh. He gasped and shuddered, his still swollen and eager cock encased in a glove of gray. Behind him, he could feel his lover's thick snake-like cock slithering between the slick globes of his ass, seeking entrance to the core of his body.

A deep, slightly threatening voice rumbled at his neck, the words muffled by the sound of running water and the kisses being trailed along his shoulder. "I've ruined your life, Runt?"

Relief flooded through him like a sudden storm on the ocean. He hadn't even realized he had been on guard, looking for that last bit of assurance this was indeed his hunter gripping him tightly. His body responded to his lover's touch like the unseen mechanism that opened the space station's doors, allowing the thrill of sexual pleasure to boil up along his limbs. He flushed and squirmed, wanting more, but Talos's hold was unrelenting, giving him only enough to make him want to beg for more.

Aidan groaned, part from being caught cursing Talos out, and part from relief his lover was there. He relaxed back into the hunter's grip and purred, "You misunderstood me, luv. Said you were the light of me miserable life. Savin' me from ruin."

Chapter Twelve

Talos's lower abdomen quivered and his snake-like cock poked up, stretching and wavering in the air, as if it knew its mate was near. It grew to its full length of fifteen inches, long and slender. The satiny-smooth, triangular-shaped tip thickened to a two-inch diameter cap ringed with firm nubs of very soft cartilage. The cap was a smoky black compared to the dusky gray of the long shaft. The opening at the very apex of the triangle secreted a clear, yellow, oily substance in a continuous, lubricating stream. Instead of a scrotum, Talos possessed a mass of six-inch long, spongy tubular appendages that surrounded his cock, masking the opening to his organ's protective pouch. His cock undulated like an exotic dancer, then retreated to its hidden burrow.

Talos carried Aidan out of the shower and directly to the massive Oracan bed in the adjoining room. By the time Aidan found himself stretched out on top of the hunter, his tanned skin was barely damp, his healing wounds clean, dry, and supple. The brand of the crest of Menalon was becoming soft and almost fully healed by Wacad's salve. Talos gently drew his thumb over the raised flesh, rejoicing in Aidan's curious but not uncomfortable expression.

"Does it still give you pain?"

"Not much. A bit of a sting." Aidan shrugged and held out a palm, then frowned. "Had rope burns scars worse. Gone now. A bit of Doc Jaclyn's magic there."

"I'm glad. For both things being gone." Talos pulled the pirate up his body until they were face to face, literally touching noses and chins. 'Ta-ti' clicked and hummed in the scant air between them. "There's been enough…challenges for one day. Enough battle." He cupped his pirate's head and sealed their lips together, exploring the taste and feel of his little lover. He could smell the lingering fear the previous challenge had left behind. He wanted to strip it away, free Aidan from its tainted hold.

As much as the pirate understood and embraced the fact he was not to blame for Jak's death, Talos had been around humans long enough to realize a part of the freewheeling, unconventional, little conman felt a measure of unwarranted sorrow over it. It was a defect in decent humans. He had seen it many times, even in Marius Webb, an experienced commander and warrior. Wacad said it was something humans called 'survivor's guilt'. Marius usually dealt with it in a few days, on his own. Talos knew Aidan would as well. He was as strong of heart as any warrior here. But it wouldn't hurt to help by giving him something else to think about.

"The only part of you that isn't marked or raw is your ass. Let me have it." Talos lifted Aidan up to a sitting position and helped the lithe body straddle his chest, Aidan's back to him.

"Not sure what ya have in mind, luv, but ay'm all for it." Aidan glanced over his shoulder in anticipation. A fevered look had already seeped into those coal black eyes.

Talos responded by shoving him forward, down on his body, the pirate's slight height making his head rest on Talos's rock-hard, defined, lower abdomen. Talos dragged the rounded ass to his mouth, spreading the bronze globes with his fingers and exposing the waiting entrance.

Ignoring the startled yip and gasp from his lover, Talos licked at the puckered bud, tracing the spidered wrinkles out from the pink center to where they disappeared into silky, smooth globes of firm muscle. It was a slow, laborious task he wanted to do again and again. The dark tang of his lover was strongest here, when the flesh was clean and warm with the lingering scent of the shower, and the fresh musk of Aidan's passionate arousal. The air was heavy with desire and need from both of them.

"Don't just knock on the door, ya torturous beast, enter!" Aidan's hands dug into to his sides, kneading and releasing, anxiety and anticipation transmitted in his trembling legs and rapid breathing.

Talos pressed the flat of his tongue to the tight hole, applying a soft, teasing pressure. Aidan groaned loudly. A small hand wormed its way between their bodies intent on the rapidly filling cock pressed into his chest. Talos let go of one succulent glob to slide his own hand up under the pirate's body, capturing his impatient lover's dick before he could.

He whispered one word, low and rough, letting the vibrations of his growly voice blow across the wet, puckered hole. "Mine." The smaller hand retreated to grasp at his side again.

The shaft was full and hot. He could feel its veins, sense the pirate's pounding pulse in the hot slender flesh. He wiped at the leaking fluid on the crown, making Aidan shudder and gasp. Now captured, he held the rod against his palm and merely flexed his fingers, massaging the straining cock, but not giving it anything more than his heated grip.

Once dominance was established, he turned back to pleasuring the clenching ass before him. Talos moved his hand to spread the hole with just the strength of his touch, widening the tight rings, making it demand he offer it relief. Sealing his mouth over the bud, he sucked hard at the flesh surrounding it, drawing his teeth in sharp bites over the tender hole. Aidan squirmed and hissed. Talos stilled him with a strong jab of a pointed tongue, letting the slick muscle glide through the open ring and rest there, like a cork in a favored bottle of brandy. He curled his tongue, its rough texture teasing the inside ring before withdrawing then reentering, a new rhythm, slow, deep and persistent. As the ring loosened, Talos began slipping his thumb alongside his tongue, letting his thick Oracan saliva provide lubrication.

Gasping oaths and dire curses, Aidan thrust his hips back, grinding his shaft into Talos's unrelenting grip and forcing his stout thumb deep into his ass. Talos removed his tongue, spitting a final dollop of lube at the widening hole. He buried his thumb to the root, searching until he found the tiny nub that made his lover yelp and bellow with pleasure.

Aidan's ass clenched hard, his cock tightened and his scrotum drew up close. The hunter could feel the cum boiling in his lover's balls, smell the rush of hormones and the sweat of desire seeping out of his quivering body. He allowed his hand to milk the straining shaft in time to his thumb's ass fucking, mentally picturing the grimace of pre-release agony on his beautiful pirate's face.

The glow from the man's flushed skin was like fire to Talos's thick, cool hide. He pressed his thumb deeper, finger fucking the wide-spread hindquarters until part of his palm slapped the stretched, burning hole. His nail flicked over the tiny rock he had been aiming for and Aidan screamed. So he did it again.

Cum dribbled over his buried, pumping fist in little splashes of creamy juice that slicked their bellies and filled the room with the musk of sex. He worked his thumb until Aidan shuddered and went limp, limbs terribly and chest heaving in a ragged, gasped dance. Talos slipped his hands away, streaking both their bodies with Aidan's release, rubbing the fluid into their pores. He craved the joining of his lover's essence with his own. It connected him to the brash, exotic, and brazen, but strangely innocent creature in ways he couldn't explain to any non-Oracan. It made Aidan literally a part of him, filling an emptiness he hadn't known was there until the pirate's cunning soul told him so.

"Seriously, luv, are I still among the livin'?" Aidan rolled off to one side, but found himself back astride Talos's body as he hit the mattress. "Whoa, mate, not got me bearings yet!"

Now he faced toward his mate, Aidan's pulsing ass nearly astride the mass of quaking tubulars that covered Talos's groin, sheltering his talented, prehensile cock. "Good. That was just the rehearsal party. This is the wedding night festivities."

Talos moved the pirate a few more inches directly onto the large nest of long tubulars. Dozens of their cupped ends teased at Aidan's still fluttering hole, latching on to suck the tender flesh. Dozens more crept upward, finding an anchor point at the base of the pirate's reawakening shaft.

"Ay'll not argue the way of it, for sure," Aidan grunted in pleasure, eyes closing momentarily, breathing labored and quick. "But the weddin's not for a few days yet, luv. Don't think the family will approve." He sagged forward, palms landing on the hunter's chest, instinctively caressing the hard, but sensitive cartilage plates under his hands.

Breathing deeply to pace their play, Talos shook his head. "Doesn't matter. We are mated, no matter the outcome of the ritual." He caressed the bounty band on Aidan's wrist with a thumb, warming the metal until it glowed. "Our connection is stronger than any ancient ceremony, deeper than a blood bond. We are no longer Oracan and human. We are warrior to warrior, forever entwined by our spirits." He curled his body, drawing his knees up to support Aidan's back. He lifted his upper body higher onto the pillows so that he could easily reach the proud, dark shaft bobbing up from his lover's groin. "Now it is time for our bodies to be so as well."

Aidan hung on, riding out the position change, mouth forming a soft "ohh" as the hunter gently stroked his firm cock. "Know he's at attention, luv, but not sure he can fire." He rocked his hips into Talos's grip despite the claim.

"He'll fire. I know how to load the gun." Talos ran his free hand through the tubular appendages behind Aidan. His cock erupted from the pouch under the tubular mound. Taking a firm hold of his quivering shaft, he directed it to his pirate's relaxed and ready hole.

Aidan's eyelids twitched and lifted, that long, low "ohh," changing to "Aye, sea serpents be gods, ohhhhhhh, bloody hell!" It rattled out of his panting, swollen lips again and again until the fifteen-inch cock had wormed its way fully into his lover's welcoming channel. It wasn't until his own shaft was being manhandled oddly that Aidan looked at him.

"Lean forward." Talos aimed the pirate's cock at the tubular nest under the base of Aidan's sex. The long strands of tubes parted, revealing a small section of open pouch. Talos grabbed his lover's hips and growled, "Lean down." When Aidan didn't move, he curled forward until the pirate's cock head nudged the opening.

Aidan grunted as the shift in his body intensified the angle of the writhing snake up his ass. Talos made his cock dance and thicken, forcing its host to fall forward at the abrupt thrust. A flush of delight darkened the tanned skin and Talos smiled at the seductive, fiery stare his lover flashed him. The runt liked the bite of rough play at times. A pirate's world, he'd learned.

But this was not a battle. It was surrender. For both of them.

"Entwined in all things, forever as one." One hand steadied Aidan's lithe frame while the other tangled in the beaded strands of thick, black hair. He tilted Aidan's head so he could watch his lover's expression. "Join with me."

§ § § §

The snake slid into his opening with a practiced ease, the undulating cock thickening once it was past the tight ring of his pucker, pressing on his every nerve, and filling his insides with a delightful heaviness he never tired of. It was as if his mate had crawled inside him, body and soul. He was sure the long snake could reach to his heart. It rubbed his sensitive channel walls, coiled and knotted over until he felt full to bursting, burning desire and need into his very core. It thrust and jabbed, entering his tight hole then leaving, burning anew at each push, then demanding Aidan beg for more. Which he did, over and over.

Impaled of the sacred totem pole of his hunter's sex, Aidan prayed to gods and demons alike that this glorious Ceme god would never desert him. He moaned and babbled, his skin flush with the rush of boiling blood that only his sea beast's flood of rich, soothing cum could quench. He wanted to ride the hardness in his ass, milk it with his body, suck it dry with his clenching channel, bury it so deep it would never find its way out.

His body grew restless. His mouth longed to taste the brandy of Talos's kiss, the forceful questing of Oracan tongue bathing his palate, stealing his air, leaving his lips raw and swollen with blissful lust. He loved to hear the special 'ta-ti' Talos clicked and hummed in his ear, his own sea serpent song of love and longing. They were his favorite alien words.

They stood next to his new favorite human words Talos had just uttered. "Join with me."

The pirate refused to wonder at the bizarre makings of the huge warrior's body that allowed it to have both dangly outside bits and hidden inside pieces. It was just one more disturbing, but primal and thrilling, thing about his hunter. Needing no further urging, Aidan lowered his upper body in small degrees, mindful of the pulsing, limber organ anchoring his ass to the hunter. The tubulars stretched to accommodate his movement, their bitey little sucking actions stinging and pulling, spurring Aidan's senses into overdrive.

Talos's cock grew thick and he felt the nubbed hood that surrounded the bulbous head flare out to anchor itself deep inside him. Lightning rippled up his spine, running like rivulets of fire around his body, entwining in his lower gut to lay at the root of his own dripping rod. It rolled there, hot and heavy, waiting to erupt in flaming passion. The need to join with his mate was overwhelming him, driving him harder, vibrating through his very bones.

Warily watching the hunter's expression for fear of doing this wrong, he rubbed the weeping tip of his shaft over the opening, gasping and panting when the edges of it curled up and sucked him down like a waiting mouth, moist and silky soft. The pouch was oddly cool, a startling sensation on his hot, blood-filled cock. He felt tight bands caress his length, massaging it, drawing it in until the entire stem was engulfed in its undulating grip.

He started a slow thrust and jab, egged on by pure primal instinct, and limited by Talos's fat, engorged member. His ass ached with the heavy fullness, Talos's embedded cock tight in his hole, stretching the small puckered opening, while the rough-edged cock-collar raked his inner flesh with each thrust of his hips. His hunter's pouch sucked his shaft, milking it with delicious, rippling bands of muscle. His body squirmed with need, every fiber sizzling, every nerve swollen and hot, he felt plugged, pulled and twisted, licked and bitten. Just when he thought he couldn't stand one more sensation, calloused fingers tugged his erect nipples, milking the tiny nubs like a goat's udder, rolling the hard titties into flaming peaks, then pinching them, forcing more moans and gasp from his panting lips.

Aidan pumped and rocked his hips, reveling in the ache and sizzling burn in his ass and his cock. Suddenly liquid filled his gut, bathing his inside channel with the hunter's cum, chill and viscous, clinging to his inner lining. He could imagine it invading his flesh, rolling fire erupting like a volcano in his gut. It rumbled up his torso to engulf every cell in his body. His heart wanted to explode in the fiery storm engulfing him.

A rush of coolness surrounded his thrusting cock. A ring of muscle teased the underside of his swollen cock, the very tip sucked and bathed in slick coolness. As his mind exploded along with his cock, Aidan fell forward into waiting hands. He screamed, a low, primal cry of completion, full of agony and nirvana like bliss. He had never heard himself make such a sound, but he wanted to make it again and again, wanted his mate 'entwined' with him just like this every time.

He doubted he could survive it, but he was willing to try.

Chapter Thirteen

At nightfall, High Principle Zeban officially declared Aidan of Menalon as having passed the first set of challenges in the Ritual of Toget.

Only the security officer Dagi challenged the ruling. Stol and Tobi were content to accept it. All had been made aware of Jak's death and the circumstances surrounding it. None disputed the judgement of a fair death. Talos was off being spiritually cleansed or some such heathen ceremony. Aidan felt alone and exposed in this circle of giant beasts, all like great turtles, sea serpents and fire breathing dragons.

Dagi had other objections though. He stepped into Aidan's personal space, towering over the slight figure.

The pirate didn't bat an eye at Dagi's unspoken threat. He'd stared down smug naval officers, powerful merchants and entire ship's crews, not to mention his own hulking sea beast. Dagi made Aidan cautious, but not afraid.

"The tasks were incomplete." Dagi's stare was tight, filled with obvious hatred and scorn for the pirate. "The human deviated from the challenge's course."

"Scudder that, matey!" Aidan swept his bare arm out to the right, gesturing at some far-off point in the night sky. He didn't know where they had been last night, but his anchor, the star of Men'lon, was in a different position then last night. That meant they were very far from last night's fateful race. "Who needs ta find a cave an' a cliff *then* a gorge if he finds the gorge first, I ask? Need ta use ya wits next time, matey, not just your muscles."

Dagi's gray complexion gained a charcoal tint, his hands slowly balling into loose fists at his side. "You did not accomplish all elements of the stated challenge." Dagi persisted, ignoring Zeban's open handed gesture to end the argument.

Stepping closer, Aidan poked at the lumbering warrior with two fingers, well aware he was touching sensitive receptors on the other male's now puffed up chest. "Not true." He let his fingers stroke the exposed breast plate under them, a light, teasing tap. "Have your facts a bit scrambled, mate. The challenge 'twas, and I quote the High Principle in command." He indicated a watchful Zeban with a flutter of his poking fingers.

Dagi's flared nostrils wrinkled at Aidan's scent. The Oracan stepped back a pace, breaking contact.

Aidan continued, "Meself just needed *'ta be first ta reach the top of the cliff's ledge where the next part o' the challenge awaited.'*" He grinned at the murmuring crowd of witnesses and challengers alike. "Did that. *Won.*"

Still irritated, Dagi charged, "You did not heed the rules."

"Aye!" Aidan spread his arms wide and smugly proclaimed, as if that answered everything clearly, *"Pirate."* Throwing Zeban a conspiratorial glance, he added in a loud whisper, "Seriously, gov, I don't know how many times I hav' ta say it."

"Jak died because of this *pirate.*"

"Jak died—" Zeban suddenly transformed from the calm diplomat to threatening Oracan warrior faster than Aidan could snap his fingers. He stepped between the security officer and Aidan, finishing his sentence through bared teeth. "As a result of his lack of honor." The warning hung in the air. Demonstrating a lack of honor during the Ritual of Toget had consequences.

Sobered by the dark change in atmosphere, Aidan spoke in a loud, but respectful voice to everyone in the arena. "I be a freeman with a pirate's code of conduct. I be neither a harlot nor a strumpet.

I'll not be taken by one not of me own choosing."

The number of witnesses had grown from last night. Many attended to witness the unique, irreverent, but clever human that the revered Hunter, Talos of Menalon, had shattered all Oracan tradition with, by finding himself trapped by their own biological imperative genetic snare. It was unimaginable, but the tiny human had outsmarted four challengers and even disposed of a hunter. The audience hummed and growled. Aidan took it as approval.

Talos had told Aidan the first witnesses had come to see him fail. Tonight's audience may have come with more charitable intentions. Aidan idly mused if there was a gent among them with which he could make a bet on his own odds of accomplishing the ritual.

His ass still throbbed with a delicious ache, his cock spent and content. His energy seemed to ebb and flow at strange times since being in this dry land, but he blamed the strange meats and spiced drinks the Oracans consumed. It wasn't the first time a bit of raw meat or a spoiled fruit had emptied his gut. It wasn't worth mentioning, but it was irritating to have it grip his bowels in the middle of this fancy tournament. He reminded himself not to eat before the next game of cunning.

Shoulders pressed back so he stood to his full height, Aidan took a deep breath and faced Zeban. He needed this to be over before his gut betrayed him again. "What's ye pleasure, your lordship? Let's hoist anchor an' set sail."

Again, the same ritual chant and declaration set the challenge into motion. "As Talos of Menalon's declared mate in the sacred Ritual of Toget, The Joining, Aidan of Maymon, come forward. You must present your sacrifice to the bond." Zeban indicated a stone near the fire pit for Aidan to sit on.

Aidan sat, silently allowing a scarred, older Oracan that Zeban announced to be a scribe instantly tattoo a swirling pattern of dots and star like black marks to his branded shoulder. The effect was a burst of fireworks falling from the healing shield of Menalon.

Aidan chuckled drily to the silent scribe. "Not so much pain in the doin' as letting Murdering Mary ink a man's flesh. Thank ye, sir." The older Oracan stood mute then gave a small bow and left the platform. The watching crowd chirped and hummed at this, but Aidan was too preoccupied by the dull throb spreading down his bicep to notice the reaction. The pain was tolerable, but hindered his upward arm movement. "Blimey! Needed 'nother stone 'round me neck."

Muttering to himself, Aidan grew somber, "Least ways, this night 'ill be one scurvy mate less." His hand fell to the hilt of the ornate knife at his waist. He'd touched it a dozen times this evening, reassuring himself it was secure and handy, letting the smooth, cool metal remind him of his lover's skin. The small, sharp blade, a bonding gift from Talos, was the only reason he was still alive. He wouldn't be forgetting that anytime soon. Marius was going to have a devil of a time keeping it from him once they returned to the station.

The heavy metal bong rang out its eerie tune. Once more, the challenge had begun.

The challenge was straight forward if daft. There was a vast maze to be run. Zeban said it covered land a thousand times the size of the enormous ritual arena. The maze was filled physical obstacles and unseen dangers. There were weapons hidden along the way, if one was resourceful enough to find them, that might help in the journey. Each entrant in the challenge would enter at a different point on the far side of the maze. Their paths would join up at some juncture. All would be the same distance away from the goal, ending at the ritual arena they now stood in.

Above, his dragon star shone brightly on his left, the glittering tip at the end of a serpent's tail in the night sky. Aidan memorized the location relative to the slivered twin moons, warmed by the sight of a friend adrift in the heavens just like he was now. He'd been studying the night sky each evening during his challenges and he now had his bearings straight, even in this foreign land.

This time when the transporter beam tingled his skin and froze his wind in his throat, Aidan peeked a look through squinted eyelids. The shimmer that surrounded him was shiny as gold, but it left him nauseous and dizzy. "Not fond that!" Arriving at his destination, Aidan called out into the empty night. "Got ta remember to talk with

Tals about that."

The surrounding land had changed, a steep wall stood to his left, a large opening, dark and unwelcoming greeted him. He was alone. A bitterness rose up in his throat and he heaved into the yellow sand at his feet. When he could talk again, he bellowed at the empty darkness. "Da ya hear me, scurvy dogs? Not fond of it a'tall!"

Sagging back, he leaned into the stone wall, the faint coolness of the rock leeching some of the heat from his now fevered flesh. Purposely, he rolled his new tattoo across the wall, sighing with pleasure when the burning sting lessened with the chill of it. A few deep breaths helped steady his churning gut. The weakness finally ebbed away, leaving only a bitterness in his mouth. Aidan straightened and walked through the dark archway.

Running, climbing, swimming. Navigating the maze was much like working his ship, climbing rigging, battling the salty ocean waves. He used the stars to guide him, maneuvering around dead ends, marking their entrances with piles of small rocks to prevent using them in error a second time. Once he found a wall with cracks in it, he scaled to the top as easily as if it were a journey to the crow's nest. It was faster going, but dangerous. The dim moonlight gave little illumination to the dull surface and the diameter of the maze walls narrowed precariously in places. After an hour, he found if he wanted to stay on course, he would have to return to the ground to find an opening to head east.

An hour of jogging through the complex corridors at ground level left him winded and sore. Eventually he found a spacious chunk of sandy ground almost directly under his favorite guiding star. Folding down into a crossed legged heap, back against the wall, Aidan sat for a moments rest.

Just as he decided he had better move on, a small sound alerted him someone was near. He drew his blade and tucked back more compactly into the shadows of the wall, desperately wishing his still labored breathing was less audible.

"I know you are there, pirate. You have nothing to fear from me." Tobi, Talos's old friend, a highly decorated hunter himself, stood tall in the dim moonlight. He held no weapons and his voice was low and non-threatening.

Aidan prided himself on gauging others, usually future victims to his light-fingered larceny tendencies, by the tone of their voice and cut of their jib. From the first night he had meet Tobi at the meal, he had not felt threatened by the darkly inked hunter. If anything, there was a sadness about the gent.

"Not one ta be cow-hearted, mate." Aidan leaned out of the shadows, making a show of slipping his blade back into his waistband. "Wondering what yer lingering for. Aren't ye set to out run me?"

"Maybe it is more interesting to learn about you then to defeat you." Tobi crouched low, heavily tattooed arms resting on his knees. He carried no weapons Aidan could see. That held little reassurance. If this hunter was skilled enough not to require a weapon of any kind to defeat both him and the other challengers, he was an opponent to be wary of in any pirate's book.

"Coulda got ta know each other over a cup of tavern grog, if'n that were true." Aidan rested his hand on the knife. "A rendezvous on the sly be 'afor less kind words."

"I researched Earth pirates when my friend claimed you as his property after Barlow's Detail was abolished."

"Did ye now?"

"I wanted to understand why. Talos has never needed or wanted to be beholden to another. It is the way of Hunters." That sadness was there. Aidan could practically taste it in the air.

"Pirates, too. Mostly." Aidan slid a little further out of the shadows. "Adventure, treasure, a wench in every port, if'n a body be lucky. A pirate's life be that." He looked up at the clear night sky and murmured, "Miss it now an' again, I do." When Tobi remained unnerving still, staring at him hard, an unreadable expression on his chiseled lizard like face, Aidan shifted so his legs were under him, primed to fight if the mood changed quickly.

"Would you like to go back to it?" It was a simple question, but Tobi's tone made it more of an offer than a casual query. "Back to adventure and treasure?"

"Why ask such a thing?"

Tobi studied the darkness around them for a moment until he said, "Talos is a warrior, a Hunter. He has achieved much, sacrificed much for the honor of his people and their culture. His reputation is unmatched in Oracan society." Only then did he look the pirate in the eye. "A rogue mate, an offworlder, a human offworlder lessens his honor."

"Rattles your sabers, does it? That I be human or pirate?"

Tobi shook his head and almost appeared to smile. "Before this ritual, I thought all humans were frail and helpless. You, pirate, have shown yourself to be a warrior. A small, easily injured one, but a warrior, quick, resourceful and intelligent." He shook his head again. Gone was the small smile. "Being pirate or human does not matter. That you are not Oracan does. Talos deserves a mate as mighty as he is."

"You applyin' for the chore, mate?" Aidan thought he might have discovered the reason for Tobi's sadness.

Tobi ignored the question. "Take my offer. Return to your own time on Earth. Leave, now before the bonding is complete. You will never have to face Talos."

"You willin' ta whisk me away? Ta break the Hunter's code?" He studied the others expression, adding, "Heard pining fer a heart 'tweren't yours be harsh on a soul. Never pined for none 'til Talos. The beastie saved me life first second we lay eyes on each 'ther." His chest ached at the thought of the monstrous beast right now. He'd never be able to leave his mate behind. "He's been savin' it ever since, keepin' me heart an' soul sane in this strange world of rules an' magic an' sailin' through the stars."

Aidan loosened the blade from his sash just a bit, preparing for any possibility. "He's right honored ta 'ave a friend what wants him proud for his people." Aidan slowly stood, ready to escape. "But me place is with Tals. Never leavin' of me own free will, mate."

"You are sure of your decision?"

"Aye, I'll not leave his side any more than he would leave mine. Ay'll give no quarter on that, matey." He felt the coolness of the wall at his back. Edging away, he continued to his right until the wall disappeared and the open archway presented itself. "We'll cross swords if needed, Hunter."

Tobi made a low unhappy sound deep in his chest, then slowly stood, towering over Aidan. He studied the pirate's face, violet eyes boring into coal black ones so long Aidan thought the hunter had fallen into a stupor. He reached out to touch the still chest when Tobi suddenly blinked.

"There will be no weapons needed between us. I can smell the bond between you and Talos, it is already too strong for it to end incomplete. You are who the snare has chosen for him. That is the way of Oracan. I cannot undo a genetic imperative." His broad shoulders slumped a fraction. "Do not be offended by my offer. I had to try. Talos is important to our people." He looked puzzled for a moment then added, "Maybe you are important to Oracan, too, pirate."

"Doubt that, mate, but 'tis grand of ye to give it mention."

"The wisdom of the Toget is vast. You might be surprised."

"Aye, that I would." Aidan brushed Tobi's serious words off, ignoring the compliment. Imagining he had some predestined greatness in him for a land he shouldn't even be in was too outrageous for the pirate to even contemplate. A pirate's life was simple and he liked it that way.

Walking to the wall on the far side of the dark archway, the hunter crouched a bit, offering Aidan his linked hands as a stirrup to lift him up. "I'll give you a head start. Use the wall as much as you can. I had to run extremely hard to catch you. Stol is more sly then he is fast, but Dagi is close. He will kill you if he can."

"That, we agree on, matey." With nothing to lose, Aidan jumped into the offered leg up and hoisted himself, crack by tiny crack, to the top of the wall. With a slap-dash salute, he was gone into the night.

Chapter Fourteen

The wall ended abruptly a few miles later. It joined a stone building that appeared eons old to Aidan. There was no option but to weave his way through the crumbling rooms, navigating rock slides and wide cracks in the ground that ran for yards and yards. Most were too wide to cross, though Aidan managed to roll a downed stone column no massive Oracan could have traversed without breaking, over one very wide and long opening, saving him at least an hour's travel.

He spent several minutes hunched over the pillar steadying it in place, so it wouldn't move once he was on it. Once that was accomplished, he finally stood up abruptly and hopped onto the makeshift bridge. Behind him, in the spot he had just vacated, the air shimmered and turned golden. A faint humming sound lingered in the air when the light disappeared, taking a few rocks and sand with it. It was odd, but he had no time to ponder it. Dagi was on his hindquarters. He needed to move.

He made sure to roll the small stone bridge into the ravine after he gained the other side just in case he had misjudged its strength. No need to give the others an advantage.

It was a simple task to set a course by the stars again from here. He had found none of the hidden items Zeban had said were offered along the way through the maze, but neither had he looked for them. The stars and his own talent for getting out of tight spots served him well enough. He needed no added baubles or tools to weigh him down. All he needed awaited at the end of the maze.

Two hours later, weary with a powerful thirst, he emerged to find Zeban seated on a stone bench, deep in conversation with Arco. On the lower level of the arena stood the audience of witnesses, more than there had been earlier. It was becoming crowded. A chant rose up from the stoic body of observers, a low, humming, guttural chirping, which was amazing and unnerving to the pirate.

At the sound, both of Talos's brothers stopped talking and rushed to Aidan.

"What has happened?" Arco impulsively touched Aidan's shoulder. "How did you get here?"

"Ran the maze." Aidan was confused. "Did the challenge, guv. Like you told me."

"You were not expected for hours." Arco and Zeban exchanged worried glances. "The course is not doable this quickly. The area to cover is too great on foot for even the fastest Oracan."

"Ohh, that. Didn't use the ground much."

"Transport devices are forbidden." Zeban grew alarmed.

"No magical boxes to move me around out there." Aidan chuckled at Zeban's obvious joke. "No little flying disc thingies either." He glanced around at the confused faces of the brothers and the audience realizing he need to explain. "Ay skinnied up the cracks in the walls an' walked on the ledge. Just like running the boom, mates. Sailed along at a good clip too. More moonlight up there." He heaved a sigh, sweat beaded on his naked torso now that the adrenaline in his system was ebbing. "Twasn't fair to the others, really. The course's made for hulking dragons and sea serpents." He grinned and swaggered a bit. "Never thought you'd be up against a smaller, lighter, quicker challenger, I'll wager."

"No, little pirate, we did not." Zeban turned to the witnesses and announced, "Aidan of Menalon has completed the second challenge with speed, intelligence and stamina worthy of the house of Menalon."

The chanting started again, a lower more throbbing version of the wordless song. While enjoying the attention and eerie homage,

Aidan was obviously lagging. He reached to steady himself on a stone column as a wave of nausea rolled through him. He felt the fever rising and the dry air was suddenly thin. "Think you could find a cuppa grog, mate? 'Tis bloody hot on this rock."

§ § § §

Talos greeted Aidan in the central room of his father's cashe. "Runt!" Talos expected Aidan to jump into his arms but the pirate dove at his chest, arms encircling as much of his broad girth as his short human arms could. Aidan buried his face in his weapons sash, an alarming amount of heat radiating through to his cool skin. "Your fever is back."

"Don't feel so good, luv." Aidan gave his lover a pleased grin. "Won, in case ya interested."

"Smart money was on you, runt." His own spiritual challenge had been endured without incident. He had finished just moments before his pirate and his brothers arrived.

Now he gave Arco a question glance as he guided Aidan to a massive couch and settled him onto it. He wiped a sheen of sweat off Aidan's clammy forehead. He pinned Arco with a worried glance. "I didn't expect you for hours. What happened?"

"Nothing. You pirate finished the course in record time." A small smile tugged at the corner of his mouth. "Apparently, our challenges do not take into consideration that a lighter, quicker challenger might entered. He scaled walls, climbed limbs and bridges to shorten his path that would not hold the weight of the other challengers." Arco actually laughed lightly. "I suspect his knowledge of navigation by the constellations helped him, as well. Zeban stayed behind to await the challengers and break the news to them."

"I knew your conniving pirate wits would finally come in handy someday." Talos stroked a meaty palm over Aidan's bare chest, enjoying the presence of the man, but alarmed at the heat radiating of the scarring flesh.

"Need a drink. Tongue's glued to me mouth like ay been lickin' tar paper. Air don't seem to hav' enough…air in it." Talos could tell Aidan didn't know what words to use but his meaning was clear. He was having trouble breathing.

Just then Pena appeared with a cup of liquid, she handed it off to Talos with a scowl for both him and his mate. Talos returned her dark stare, saying, "Wacad's in with Menalon. Get him. Quick." Talos didn't worry about the harshness of his tone. Pena had worked in this house for decades. She was used to all the ways of the cashe.

"Don't know if it matters, but there be strange lights in the night, in the maze. All sparkly and golden-like. Only lasted a few second, then it were gone. Right where I were standing but a moment afore." He drew in a ragged breath that made him cough, heavy lids drooping as he rambled on. "Sounded like bees. Whole nest of the stinging buggers. Wondered if it was a trap I should be avoiding here. What think ya, me gorgeous beastie?"

"It's trouble, runt. Stay away from anything like that for now, okay? You jake with it?" Talos darted a worried glance at Arco, who nodded out of Aidan's sight.

"'m good, luv. Just need that drink. Stomachs all a churnin' like ay swallowed a whoppin' great Kracken."

Talos held the cup to Aidan's dry lips. He only took a small sip before the pirate heaved it back up. When he caught his breath, he whispered to Talos, "No offense to the good Doc Waca, but been missin' Doctor Jaclyn in a fierce way, sharp tongue and all."

Wacad rushed into the room with Pena, who lingered in the background. "Menalon is recovering, slowly but recovering. What's happened?"

"That's three times he's chucked his lunch while on Oracan." He ticked each new item off on his fingers. "Oracan planet, Oracan snare, Oracan bonding ritual. One or all of them are making him sick. He needs Oracan medicine. Are you still refusing to help figure out what's up with him?"

"I'm not refusing, Talos. I'm obeying Oracan law. You live by our laws more than any of us. You know there are limits to what I can do without full Council approval. Approval that was denied."

"Fine." He gently lifted Aidan off of the couch. "I'm contacting P6. Sending for the doc there. If you won't treat him, a human doctor needs to." He strode out of the room leaving a heavy silence behind him.

§ § § §

"How would you like to take a trip with me," Marius walked around Dr. Jaclyn Rice's work station and whispered in her ear, "I promise it will be an experience you won't regret."

The doctor turned her startling green eye on her lover and smiled, a seductive twinkle in her expression. "Will it be romantic?"

"Hmmm." Marius hesitated, then walked around the station to face her. "Not exactly. It will be warm and sunny, but those are actually some of the bad points."

"Okay." She wrinkled her forehead in a frown. "Where is this less than idyllic vacation spot and why would we go there?"

"Oracan. Because Talos asked us to, actually asked *you* to go." He ran through the brief conversation he just had with the hunter and revised his answer. "Demanded really. More like an order."

"That overgrown rhino is—"

He attempted to placate her with raised hands of surrender. "Aidan's ill. Really ill and not improving. The Oracans refuses to do anything but first aid because he's not an Oracan. The little spitfire has been showing them all what he's made of, but its taking a toll. He need a doctor. His doctor who knows him."

"Me."

"You. And me."

"Corp Central is all right with the station commander leaving on short notice?" Jaclyn hesitated then skeptically added, "They like their stations all neat and tidy in the personnel departments. You don't have relief on board."

"They agreed to let Honeywell man the helm while I'm gone." Her mouth dropped open, surprise widening her eyes. He whispered conspiratorially, "No choice. They received the request for both of us directly from the Oracan Council High Principle Belith. Corp Central was tripping all over itself to comply. They've tried for years to open discussions with the Council over establishing outposts in Oracan territories. With zero response. They'd have sent the entire medical staff if the request had come through."

"Oh great. A political land mine with Aidan in the middle. I don't envy you." She began downloading data from the pirate's databank. "Do you know his symptoms?"

"Talos said he was transmitting everything Doctor Wacad, one of Talos's older brothers, recorded on Aidan since they arrived. You should have it," He checked a small monitor on his wrist, "Now. Aidan's throwing up. Can't keep liquids down. He passed out moments after arrival, too. They assumed it was the heat."

"When do we leave?"

"A shuttle is waiting for us in hanger bay twelve. My bag is already there."

"Give me time to stock a med pouch and grab an overnight bag and I'll meet you there."

They exited the sick bay together, but each ran off in a different direction when the doors opened.

§ § § §

Aidan awoke to the sound of familiar voices, one deep and harsh, his hunter's aggravated growl, and the other a light, snipping voice that lanced through a man's ear like a lady's hatpin when she was aggrieved about something. Apparently, the good doctor was aggrieved.

"Bit of a shrew at times, but she's worth the tongue lashings mostly." Aidan grinned at the sight of Rice sitting attentively at his bedside. Talos hovered over her shoulder like a towering, sea serpent guard. Even Commander Marius paced the floor beyond the foot of the bed.

His head throbbed, but his vision had cleared. The pit of his stomach felt emptier than it had since he'd got the runs from spoiled meat in a tavern in Port Royale during a particularly hot summer. Everything on the islands had gone rancid that season. The thought produced a slight wave of nausea, but he was able to force it down. There was one more challenge for him to face and he intended to show these brutish beasts just what a pirate was made of. He'd not be bringing dishonor to the house of Menalon and his lover. He'd endure whatever he had to and finish the bonding ritual that meant so much to these primal creatures. Honor and winning were a fine and fancy thing, but all he wanted was Talos. That would be his treasure for a lifetime.

And he needed Doctor Jaclyn to make it so.

"Well, you're feeling better." She pressed a cool hand to his forehead, sparing a glance at Talos as she told him, "Fever's broken, for now."

"Just the sight of your lovely face has cured my ills, m'lady." He gave her a genuine shy smile and added softly, "Missed your tatterin' an' chidin' me. Got too much to bear. Made me ill, it did."

"Too bad it doesn't tie your tongue down." She pressed a thin stick to his arm and he felt nothing but the chill of the metal and the smoothness of the tip against his skin. "His vital signs are normal, but his blood chemistry still needs monitoring. He'll need to be moved." She looked across the wide bed at a group Aidan hadn't noticed before. She stood up, fists balled on her shapely hips. "I'm assuming you have a medical center here, Doctor Wacad."

Wacad and Zeban drew closer. "Yes," the healer paused to choose his words diplomatically, "But it is not equipped to treat humans."

"Really?" It was more of a condemnation than a question. Wisely, no one attempted to answer her. "Considering you and your Council are subjecting a human to dangerous rituals, barbaric practices like branding, and unsanitary blood rituals, along with unfamiliar foods and exposure to alien plant life, I'd expect you to be more prepared for injuries, illness, and possible allergic reactions in a human. After all, didn't the Council demand he come here and be subjected to all of this?"

"Told you the dame had a whip for a tongue." Talos replaced Rice at Aidan's side, helping the pirate to sit up against the headboard and pillows. "But she makes sense."

"Oracan law does not permit revealing biological data."

"Well, if Aidan's physiology is changing, adapting to Oracan biological elements, then Oracan biological data is what I need to figure out a diagnosis. It's pretty straight forward."

"Feeling fit as a fiddle." Aidan was anxious to put the sickness behind him. He had a challenge ahead of him soon. Why did it matter what caused it if he was better? He crawled pass his lover and stood naked at the bedside. "Knew your magic potions and voodoo spells would fix me up, Doc."

"Be quiet." Marius, Rice and Wacad all spoke in unison.

"Seeing as I'll not be needed here..." Aidan sniffed and pouted. "I'll make use of the rain closet and find me clothes. Have a challenge to win. Come with me, luv." He nudged a willing Talos to his feet and they left, heading for the bathroom.

"You can't go to the challenge, Aidan. You need to rest," Dr. Rice call out.

"Already gone, m'lady. I'll not quit 'til it be done or I be gone. There's no fighting it, lass, me honors at stake." The door closed on her before she could respond.

§ § § §

Rice turned her frustration on the remaining Oracans. "Seriously, Councilmen, you can't ask us to travel all this way to help and then refuse to cooperate. Aidan is improved, for the moment, but he's been getting progressively worse each day here. Whether it's the stress of the ritual, severe dehydration, or these mysterious genetic changes he's undergoing, the answer lies in our working together."

"Aidan has not asked for Oracan help. He asked for you," Zeban gently reminded her.

Rice's cheeks tinged pink and she dug her fists into her hips.

"Aidan is an innocent in an alien world he's hasn't had time to understand. For Jupiter's sake, he hasn't caught up to the nineteenth century on Earth let alone an entire alien culture seven hundred years ahead of him."

"We accept his gap in universal knowledge." Zeban's calm voice and passive demeanor only seem to irritate the doctor.

"Well, accept this. This bonding fever is unnatural for a human. We aren't equipped to deal with it. Here he is isolated, no friends, no family, thrust into a warrior culture unlike anything he can relate to."

"Aidan has friends here, Dr. Rice. And family."

Marius stepped forward a pace. "Maybe we should take this discussion to another room? Have a seat, talk reasonably about what can be done, by both parties to work out the issues." Marius opened the bedroom door and stood waiting expectantly.

Rice ignored the offer. "Of course, Aidan didn't ask for Oracan help. He hates doctors. He doesn't know what to ask for! He has no idea what Oracan medicine can do for him. And neither do I *because* you won't share your knowledge. Pretty cold for a people professing to take him into their society."

Wacad sighed. With a resigned glance at Zeban he relented a small margin, "Take blood and tissue samples from him. I'll analyze them when I run Menalon's most recent samples." Wacad addressed his brother. "He's improved but not as quickly as the young pirate has."

"Wait. Someone else is sick in the same house?" Rice dropped her fists and looked from Zeban to Wacad and back. "What are the symptoms? Who is ill?"

"Menalon, our father, took ill the night Talos and Aidan arrived. It was serious for a period but he has much improved. His complaints were not like Aidan's."

"Symptoms of a disease can manifest differently in different species. You know that, I'm sure. We see it all the time on P6 with all the intergalactic travelers and species we get. It could be the same cause as Aidan's illness if his doesn't turn out to be bonding side effects. What's Menalon's diagnosis?"

"We are uncertain as of yet." Wacad grudgingly admitted. "It is an unknown agent that has invaded his organs."

"What are you treating him with? We need to test Talos as well to compare with Aidan's if it is related to your bio-chemical bonding process." The conversation shifted to research, medical discoveries, diagnoses and laboratory findings. At last a common ground was established between the doctors, human and Oracan.

Marius heaved a sigh of relief and sat down to await Talos and Aidan's return. The doctor was going to need specimens from both of them.

Chapter Fifteen

The chant was louder, the low, thumping voices sounding more aggressive, on the last evening of the Ritual of Toget. It vibrated the air, echoing inside Aidan's chest, rattling his rib cage and burrowing deep into the pit of his stomach. He had come to enjoy the sing-song rhythm and throaty base. It was like his former shipmates cheering him along in a tavern brawl. He found a comfort in the thought of it.

This final task would end the ritual. It would seal his fate as Talos's mate and put an end to the troubled scowl that had settled on his lover's ugly Oracan face of late. Talos was quieter, less talkative around his family. Broodier. The hunter worried too much.

His brooding hunter stood tall and proud on the edge of the platform. Aidan's blade poked out of the hunter's weapons sash, alongside the matching one. Aidan wasn't allowed to have it for this challenge. Restricted by Oracan law from being beside Aidan during his previous challenges, ritual now demanded Talos be present when the final challenge was completed. It was then that the blood bond would be performed, binding them together for all time.

There was a fierceness, a primal attitude of possession and ownership radiating from the stoic hunter that Aidan found hypnotic. A mere glance from his lover set his cock throbbing and his ass clenching in anticipation of the coming celebration. Aidan planned on spending all of it astride his monstrous lover's serpent cock. He had to look away for fear his own growing shaft would interfere with the task at hand. There was work to be done. Challengers to defeat.

Aidan was enjoying the ritual. The games, the challenges to his wits and body, the warm air on his skin and the wind at his back. But he was also anxious to return to their home floating in the stars and their more carefree life. Wherever they were, life with the hunter was not boring.

Tonight was no exception.

The night air was thin and dry, smelling faintly of oil from the multitude of flicking torches that lit a circle within the arena. Aidan stood alone while Tobi, Stol and Dagi awaited instructions for the final challenge of the ritual. Zeban wasted no time by taking center stage.

"As Talos of Menalon's declared mate in the sacred Ritual of Toget, The Joining, Aidan of Maymon, come forward. You must present your sacrifice to the bond." Zeban indicated the stone near the fire pit for Aidan to sit on.

Aidan stood, bared upper torso, a thin red sash tied around his forehead to hold back his thread-twined and beaded hair. Energy coursed through his lithe frame, adrenaline hyping his sense of excitement, battling back the dull heaviness in his stomach. The sickness had improved since Dr. Jaclyn had used her voodoo skills on him. A long shower with his lover had helped erase the pent-up tension in his groin, the sex hard and fast and satisfying. Now, he was ready for whatever these beastly giants were to throw at him next.

The same scarred, older Oracan scribe waited by the stone bench, his curious tattooing device held at the ready.

The pirate greeted the scribe with a nod, his hands steepled together in a praying gesture, showing respect and admiration to the elder. He added a little bow, returning the Oracan's gesture of last night. A barely perceptible head nod acknowledged him.

Aidan sat and the scribe immediately applied the device, this time lower on his arm. The marking took several applications and covered a larger area of his skin. When the scribe stepped away, a one-inch band of black encircled his upper arm, the thick strip was bordered with curls, dots and confusing alien symbols. In an elongated loop, a small ship sailed in the curled waves below one shining star.

"Right fine workmanship, guv. Thank ye." Aidan nodded at the scribe who again, bowed but this time the Oracan solemnly added, "Honor and Compassion," with the traditional Oracan arm gesture before retreating. Aidan returned the vow and the witness gallery's chant became nearly deafening.

Straining to look at his new tattoo more fully, Aidan grinned at the ocean vessel, pleased a piece of his own life had been added to the intricate, alien design. His arm ached more than the night before, but the pride of having his pirate self acknowledged was worth it all.

Moving close to Zeban, Aidan whispered, "The crowd likes your scribe fellow. Don't talk much, but he's right good at his job." He showed the Councilman his newly marked arm with pride. "Looks a bit like me old ship, she does."

Zeban smiled. "Shelar of Ak has been our scribe, much like your monks, for as long as I have been alive. And he never speaks or bows to any ritual member, chosen or challenger." He glanced to the chanting witnesses, a unified voice both strong and fierce. "A great honor has been bestowed upon you, little pirate. A great honor."

Flexing his branded arm, Aidan grinned. "I be acceptin' the honor." He threw a calculating stare at his remaining challengers. "What's your pleasure this night, guv?"

Zeban stepped back and addressed the waiting challengers. "The Ritual of Toget's final challenge will pit the chosen one against a single challenger."

Removing a rough gray box from his robe, he presented each Oracan with the box. All three removed an identical stone from the box. The palm sized rock glittered, the firelight reflecting off their fine sand particles that shone like diamonds.

One by one at Zeban's direction, Stol, Tobi, and finally Dagi, tossed their stones into the fire pit. Only one exploded into a flame of green and gold.

Sharing a quick, uncomfortable glance with Talos, Zeban announced, "Dagi of Meollege has been granted the challenge of personal battle. Dagi, declare your weapon of choice."

"As you command, High Principle Zeban." Eyes fever-bright

in the light of the dozens of torches surrounding the arena battle ground, Dagi strode to a waiting security guard carrying a wooden box. "I choose the *benii*, the ancient sword of our first hunters, a symbol of our honor and compassion."

Taking pleasure in the stunned silence of the crowd, he pulled the sword from the holder, the wide blade glowing in the bright moonlight. Its handle was thick and oddly shaped. Aidan suspected his hand wouldn't even fit around the hilt. The obvious weight of the weapon was evident in the way Dagi's bicep bugled and strained.

"I present a pair of benii for the ritual." Dagi replaced his sword in the box and presented it to Zeban. "The chosen may pick which one he would like to use. Both are fine weapons."

"That will not be necessary." A thunderous, deep, growling voice pierced the night, parting the crowd as its owner marched through the arena. Menalon climbed to the ritual platform, followed closely by Wacad and a burly personal guard. "The chosen one has his own benii, one handed down through the ages by family." He opened the ceremonial box to remove a similar sword, this one slightly smaller and lighter. He presented it to Aidan, confiding in a low voice, "It belonged to my mate, Etta. I, too, had to battle many challengers for the right to bond with her. May it serve you well, tiny pirate."

Aidan reverently accepted the blade, the hilt was thick but flowed thinner in places well enough he found a good grip. "Thank ye, Men'lon. Owned by a dragon! Powerful spirit, to be sure." He caressed the blade like it was the finest sword he had ever seen.

Menalon leaned close and whispered, "Very, very old benii had a thin blade in the end of the hilt. Handy in tight battles." He locked stares with Aidan. "This is very, very old." He nodded, apparently making up his mind to add, "His is not."

Turning briskly, Menalon walked away to stand at Talos's side, a watchful, silent Wacad and his guard close at hand. It wasn't obvious, but Aidan knew Menalon was still feeling the effects of his earlier illness. The pirate sympathized with him on that.

Brandishing his new sword, tip to the ground from the weight, to get the feel of it in his hand, he turned his attention to Zeban. "Any rules to this game, guv?"

"Combatants must stay within the torch circle. No second party may assist during the battle. Battle ends when one is unable to continue fighting."

"No rules then." Aidan gave a saucy grin. He made a show of struggling to raise the heavy sword and wield it with precision. "A man can work with that."

Zeban waved Tobi and Stol to follow him out of the arena circle. Once Dagi and Aidan were alone, Zeban announced, "Let the challenge begin."

The gong sounded, eerie in the sudden stillness. The entire crowd of witnesses stood unmoving, their chant now fading on the night air, waiting. The pirate knew most expected this to be a quick fight, the tiny human no match for the Oracan warrior. It was the promise of a bloodbath that stirred their heathen souls.

Aidan rolled his head on his shoulders, loosing the tightness that had settled into them. Widening his stance to balance his weight as he turned his side to Dagi, he judged the strength of his thrusts he would need to gain the best leverage with this glorious new sword. Dagi did nothing more than stare at him, sword in hand and waiting for Aidan to make the first move.

"Do you not know what pirates do, mate? For a livin'?" He skirted around Dagi flexing his arms, gently swaying the sword still pointed at the ground as if it was too heavy to raise quickly.

"Steal, murder and cheat, I'm told." Dagi turned only his head, watching Aidan as he circled him in a slow, casual dance. He was alert and ready, but confident in his skill to win.

"Aye, some do all that, some do part. But do ye know what they do when they not be doin' those things?" Aidan had worked his way around to Dagi's less dominant side. Here he shuffled his feet in the sand, clearing away loose pebbles that might affect his ground, stare never leaving Dagi's malevolent gaze. A broad rock maybe two-foot high lay beside him.

Dagi sneered. "Gorge themselves on their stolen goods?"

"Aye, we do that." Aidan acknowledged the practice, logically adding, "No point in liberatin' treasure if'n ye don't make use of it."

"Honorless gutleggs." Dagi raised his sword, his body language shifting to a more offensive line.

Altering his grip just a hair, Aidan poked a little more at his deadly challenger. "And when a pirate fights over this wicked bounty, do ye know how we fight?"

"Like cowards?" The corner of Dagi's jaw twitched and his eyes narrowed. Aidan guessed it was a Oracan sign of amusement.

"No, mate, with swords." Aidan jumped to the nearby stone, launching himself up and at Dagi. His sword swept through the air, clashing firmly with Dagi's startled defense. The pirate spun around in tight circles, slashing and thrusting as he traveled the width of the arena. Swords scrapped and hit, gleaming in the firelight. Aidan stayed in constant motion for several minutes, working the open ground, using the surrounding rocks to gain height for leaps, forcing Dagi to defend his line.

After one successful inside jab, Dagi's blade came back bloodied. He grunted in satisfaction, showing the crimson blade to the witnesses. The audience remained oddly silent, all still intent on the final outcome.

Aidan recognized the rumble of Talos's displeasure and quickly bared his side to show a small nick in the taunt flesh. "A one count, matey." He parried a thrust and danced away from the massive blade. "You'll not get a second one."

The tempo of the fight increased. Both were equal to the task. What Dagi presented in planning, strength and height, Aidan countered with speed, dexterity and wit.

Allowing himself to be backed into a corner, Aidan fumbled his sword and Dagi pounced, knocking it from his hand. It flew off to one side, a mighty thrust that forcefully dragged it from his grasping fingers. Dagi wasted no time in dropping down over Aidan, stone-encrusted sword hilt posed to smash the pirate's face. The sheer weight of the thick hilt would do major damage, but with the force of Dagi's strength behind it, Aidan knew he wouldn't survive. He also knew from the look in Dagi's eyes there was nothing that would stop him. Almost.

Before Dagi could drive the hilt home, Aidan took the stiletto thin dagger he had pulled from the end of his sword as it was forced out of his grip and slipped it deep into the warrior's chest, at a point under his ribs where he had learned his own lover was extremely sensitive. Dagi froze, the sword falling from his trembling fingers.

Aidan rolled him off, wiggling out from under the heavy body, adding, "Think 'tis the 'compassion' part of the sayin', mate." Aidan stood up and brushed himself off, protecting his wounded side with one hand. "Not too sure about if'n this counts as the 'honor' part too."

Talos raced to the perimeter but one gesture from his father and he held his place on the sidelines. Zeban and Wacad crouched beside Dagi.

The healer looked up at Zeban. "The neural bundle has been damaged. His sensory system is in chaos. He'll recover once the blade is removed and the pathways sealed again." Wacad stood abruptly and harshly demanded an answer from Aidan. "Where did you learn Oracan physiology?"

"Fizzy what?" He rocked on the balls of his feet, fidgeting with the ever-present band on his wrist. He was tired and becoming nauseated again. It there was going to be more to the evening's events, he wished they would get on with it.

"How did you know where to injure him?" Wacad was calmer, as if patiently questioning a child.

"Oh, that. Accidentally hit Talos with a lamp right there once. Maybe twice. Can't really remember. Knocked the wind right out of 'im. Made it easier to slip by and..." Aidan's answer trailed away when he realized he wasn't willing to tell the whole story to his hunter's brothers. Best somethings be kept between lovers.

He began walking toward Talos and the others, vaguely aware Tobi was standing near Talos, but Stol was nowhere to be seen. "Sore loser, that one,'" he muttered, dismissing the nervous trade merchant from his thoughts.

Zeban followed as others joined Wacad in caring for the fallen warrior. "Figured it was me one chance at surviving this. Fine swords, but bloody heavy." He picked up the sword Menalon had given him as he passed it, gently hefting it in his grip. "Was gettin' a wee bit winded toward the end. Had to do something to end it fast."

Talos caught his eye and Aidan leapt into his love's waiting arms, arms and legs wrapping around the might Oracan, careful of the sword dangling from one hand. "Missed ye, ye bloody, hulking, sea beastie!" Heedless of the crowd pressed around them, Aidan kissed his hunter long and deep. He only broke off when Zeban cleared his throat and removed the sword from Aidan's hand.

Speaking to the witnesses, Zeban declared, "The final challenge has been met. Aidan of Menalon has honored The Ritual of Toget and earned the right of blood bonding with the hunter, Talos of Menalon." Zeban led the way out of the arena. Talos and Aidan followed.

Both of them sat at the fire pit. The chanting was replaced with a low, soothing hum. Aidan felt it vibrating in his chest, like the snare drums the British liked to beat on when they marched. It drifted on the night air, oddly in rhythm with the dry breeze that sent wisps of smoke from the fire pit swirling up to the night sky. Aidan followed a tendril of gray as it rose up, his dragon star was overhead, it glittered and winked at him. A sense of belonging crept into his soul. He tucked it away, saving it for a time when he needed it. Now, he belonged to his mate. Body and soul.

Talos presented his wrist. Zeban made a quick cut with the ceremonial knife that Talos had given Aidan. He collected the blood in a cup. Aidan watched in fascination as Talos's wound sealed over quickly, the bleeding dribbling away in mere seconds. Mimicking his mate, Aidan presented his wrist, merely blinking away the sting of the knife's blade, Talos's twin blade drawing the thick red liquid to the same cup. He needed a bit of pressure to seal over his wound.

Zeban sprinkled sand into the cup then stirred the contents together. He spoke words into the cup, Oracan words Aidan could not understand. Talos had told him to expect that, as no translation to other languages existed. They were sacred vows, ancient words, never repeated outside the blood bonding.

Zeban gave Talos the cup. The hunter dipped his fingers into it, bringing them out smeared red and he gently slathered it over Aidan's tattoo. The pirate jumped at the sudden coolness, surprised then delighted as the ink of his markings changed. The dark red filled in the spaces that had been previously left empty between the curls and dots, even making the ship's sail and night sky a brilliant crimson red. The transformation happened so quickly, Aidan was left to marvel again at the skill of the scribe who had marked him. No blood was left behind, every drop absorbed into the magical inking.

When it was Aidan's turn, he eagerly repeated Talos's performance, marveling at the changes in his lover's marks. The color was deeper, almost dark as cherries. Where the hunter's existing tattoos had been muted before, blending almost into the dark gray skin, now they stood out against the gray, a deep charcoal and ruby shade.

"'Tis beautiful an' fierce." Aidan grinned at his mate. Exhaustion had crept up as they sat, a new sharp pain had blossomed in his side. His stomach threatened to rebel against the smell of the blood. Suddenly, the air was becoming too thick to breath.

Talos nodded. "Like us." He pointed at Aidan. "Beautiful." Then at himself. "Fierce."

Any retort the pirate had was interrupted by Zeban ringing his ancient gong and proclaiming, "The blood bond is done. Aidan of Menalon has completed the Ritual of Toget with honor. Let none challenge this union blessed by the ancients and bonded by blood and Oracan law."

The sound of someone familiar calling his name registered, but Aidan was spinning too fast to focus on it. Long arms encircled him, squeezing the air out of his lungs, tentacles clawed at his mouth, blowing hot air in his face. Waves splashed over him, cold as Davy Jones's locker. Then the Kracken swallowed him whole.

It was dark and lonely in the belly of the beast.

Chapter Sixteen

"He's been poisoned."

"What? How? I know he's been sicker since he got here, but we both eat the same things, drink the same drinks." Talos stormed into the small, outer chamber of the treatment room Aidan was recovering in. "Other than the wine Menalon gave him at the meal. Pena can tell you what it was. She served it to him."

Marius and Dr. Rice worked over a small bank of portable monitors, concerned frowns marring both their faces.

"I'll need to test a few things to check on the foods, maybe it's something he's allergic to here, but this wasn't something he ate." Dr. Rice handed her findings to Marius, but Talos tore them from her hand first. "It came from his stab wound. It was shallow, barely a factor, but—"

"The sword had poison on it. Dagi pulled a fast one." Talos peered past the partially open doors to check on his mate. Aidan was sleeping, his breathing slow and regular, even now with the breather removed. Talos thought his heart had stopped when the pirate had fallen, body shaking, his chest still as the dead. Wacad had revived him with mouth to mouth. It had been several very tense moments until they arrived at the treatment center. "The dirty, cheating bastard."

Talos strode toward the exit doors that led to the rest of the medical center. "Where are you going?" Marius jumped around Dr. Rice and tried to head the hunter off.

"Where do you think I'm going? To find Dagi and remove his

beating heart." Talos thundered out into the hall.

Marius gave Dr. Rice an exasperated shrug. "Aren't you going to say anything to him?"

"Like he listens to me." Her sarcasm wasn't lost on Marius. "He'll reconsider once he finds Dagi."

"You're sure?" Marius didn't share her optimism. He knew how far the hunter would go to protect his lover.

"Wacad said Dagi is currently paralyzed, unable to move any limbs. There is no honor in taking his life. A hunter lives for honor. Plus, Dagi doesn't explain Aidan's symptoms before the challenges."

Throwing up his hands, Marius said, "I'm going with him. Just in case reason or honor isn't on his mind right now."

Dr. Rice nodded, barely looking up from her work.

§§§§

The room had a soft glow to it, shining from behind the walls. Odd humming sounds pestered his hearing like tiny bees buzzing in his ears. It smelled like soap and harsh scents that made his nose wrinkle in disgust. The berth beneath him was strange, oddly soft and lump free. There were no rough edges or crawlin' things, and it swayed in circles instead of with the pitch of his ship. The room was foreign to him, all clean and tidy, unlike any brothel he had visited in his short years.

Aidan shook his head to clear the jumbled thoughts. The vision of a sea serpent danced before his bleary eyes and slowly pieces of his recent days came back in snips and snags, a face here, a name there, the memory of a tender 'ta-ti' sound filled him with warmth. Talos. He needed to find his hunter.

He made to push himself upright off the bed when a strong hand and demon face yanked him to a standing position. "Careful, mate, ye're likely to be wearin' me super if ye be so rough." He stumbled against a hard, cold, large body, his thin, baggy trouser nearly slipping off his slender hips.

"Stand still and be quiet, pirate. I need you alive to get paid, but that's all."

The voice was familiar, he knew he should know it, but the name lingered on the outside of his thoughts. Then the room buzzed and a golden shimmering light carried him away.

§§§§

"I told you not to follow me." Talos walked through the outer office doors, fuming at Marius's interference.

"Aren't you glad I did?" The commander followed close behind his friend, determined to make him see the situation in a clear light.

"No." Talos was having no part of a reasonable discussion.

"Really? I'd have thought stopping you from committing—" Marius stopped short at sight of an empty room. "Jaclyn was right here when I left." He moved to the monitors where Dr. Rice had been working, seeing an open screen patiently awaiting commands. "She didn't look like anything could tear her away from her data banks."

Both barreled through the closed door to Aidan's treatment room nearly falling over Dr. Rice's unconscious body.

§§§§

"There aren't any options left, Zeban. Aidan is out there, taken by someone who wants him dead or worse. He's sick. I can feel him weakening through the bond, but it isn't strong enough yet to give me much to go on."

"The Council is deliberating, Talos. These things take time." Zeban sympathized.

Talos knew his brother wanted Aidan to be recognized as an Oracan citizen. He had fought and won the right, but this was all so new to Oracan. The Council was understandably reluctant to be hasty in any decision defining an offworlder's status on Oracan society.

"The dame is working on it, but she needs help."

"Hey, Talos." Marius stepped out of the corner of the room and touched the weapons sash in a brisk rub. "You know Zeban's hands are tied. He's doing all he can. Everyone is."

"What's the point of rescuing him, Marius, if he dies once he's back anyway?"

"If I had evidence to support a claim that an Oracan is responsible for Aidan's illness, that might sway the Council. As it stands now, he may have contracted a disease before he arrived here. Or it may be that humans can't tolerate mating with an Oracan. That will not be viewed as an Oracan issue."

"That doesn't change things." Talos stubbornly stood his ground. "Aidan is officially my mate. A son of Menalon. The doc can't work out how to cure him. The bond, poison, the snare, disease, whatever it is, it's twisting him up inside. It's like trying to repair a Jegsag cruiser without the engineering data. It's all guess work and any mistake can blow you and it to pieces. She needs Oracan physiology data and Wacad to help her."

The doors burst open. Wacad and Dr. Rice rushed in, each holding an injector. They were both so excited they talked over each other in a constant stream of medical language and findings.

"We found the problem." Towering over Dr. Rice, Wacad's smile couldn't compare with hers. "It's not poison, at least not like the poison Menalon was given."

"Menalon was poisoned?" The other three men exchanged startled looks.

"Definitely, but it's mild. Still have to figure out who, but he'll make a full recovery." That one poured out of Dr. Rice on a river of relief. "But the bonding's not Aidan's problem."

"He's not allergic to any Oracan foods or drink." Wacad ticked off each finding on his fingers as they talked.

"It isn't a new disease he picked up on P6. Thank Gods." Dr. Rice heaved a deep sigh of relief. "I did NOT want to have report that one to Corporate."

"How do you know all this?" Marius interrupted the constant flow between the two physicians.

"It was wonderful! Wacad presented his case to the medical Council that since Talos, Oracan's greatest and mightiest Hunter," Dr. Rice rolled her eyes at Marius, "lives on P6 with his mate, it was in Oracan's best interest that a qualified physician be near to him." She almost giggled. "They agreed to allow limited biological data sharing with me, personally, as his private home station physician. For the first time." She leaned forward and fake whispered to Marius. "Ever!"

"Are you sure you're all right, Doc? You got thumped pretty hard on your noggin." Talos watched the verbal assault like it was a ping pong game, darting back and forth between them.

"We have a cure." Dr. Rice raised her injector in the air triumphantly. "Well, not a permanent cure, but something good enough to keep him alive until he gets back here for proper treatment."

"A cure for what exactly?" Even Marius had been waiting for the big reveal.

"Wacad helped me isolate the foreign element in Aidan's blood stream that has been disrupting his cell development. It's a heavy element that has been creating tiny abscesses in his liver." Dr. Rice's eyes glowed with the excitement of the discovery.

Wacad took up the tale. "It's been being absorbed over time in very small amounts, but over time it has reached critical stages for a human body's tolerance. Dr. Rice and I believe the abscesses become irritated when Aidan is stressed or experiencing extreme exertion. They swell and ultimately burst, releasing the toxin into his blood stream. That's what is causing the sudden bouts of illness. Why it was so hard to correlate the symptoms to any outside factors."

"This still doesn't explain where it is coming from. How's it getting into him?"

Dr. Rice stepped closer to Talos. "Remember when I asked you to take the bounty band off Aidan? And you swore it would protect him?" She raised his eyebrows and tapped the hunter's chest with the injector. "Well, think again, you big palooka."

"What? That can't be the right skinny."

"It is. The element in his system is the one element, K^8, that is in the band that allows all hunters to connect with their bounty. To track them should they escape or become lost." Wacad shrugged. "Long term effects research has never been needed. No bounty wears it very long."

"Now we need to find him." Dr. Rice stared at Talos expectantly. "Find him. Use your connection and find him."

"I can't. Last time I used it, I had to grip it in my hand for it to work."

"During the branding." Zeban encouraged the hunter to explain it more clearly.

"Yeah. To help him tolerate the pain. He heard me, but something's blocking it."

"Actually, it's probably because all of the K^8 has been absorbed out of the band and into his body through his skin." Wacad studied the now useless medication in his hand. "There's not enough left on Aidan's end to bridge the connection."

A somber silence settled over the room until Dr. Rice jumped off her seat on the corner of a desk and announced, "Then let's strengthen it on this side of the connection." She gave Talos a long, hard look. "I've always wanted to see what the inside of a hunter looks like."

§ § § §

Aidan stared at the dark circle until it took form. The opening to the cave was carved into the side of a rocky steep cliff. Night was approaching. Two moons were already visible in the sky, both pale against the orange haze of the receding day. He rolled over on the warm sand, feeling the grit of the granules grate over his bare back and side. His efforts were slow, his legs refusing to do his bidding. His stomach growled, empty but queasy. Then he remembered the golden shimmering light. The one that made people and things disappear and then reappear elsewhere. This place must be his 'elsewhere'. He was less fond of the light now than before.

Aidan could see the dim outline of a massive beast. He smelled the scent of Oracan flesh near. Oracan but not his hunter. This one smelled of sweat and fear. Every pirate had a nose for fear. It told you when to fight and when to run. This one said fight if you're able. Aidan wasn't sure if there was much fight left, but he'd take his moment if it presented itself.

He drifted in and out, dreaming about great winged dragons that flew over his head in the sky, and Ceme gods soothed his thoughts with murmured hums and wordless chants. The dream left him feeling stronger, more awake. He lay where he had been earlier, surprised to see the sky was still light and the stars were not yet out. Only minutes must have passed instead of the hours he felt had slipped away.

His vision cleared enough to distinguish Stol standing a few feet away, working furiously on a handheld, triangular device, oblivious to his surroundings.

Aidan slowly moved one hand then the next, feeling the ground beneath, searching for anything that could be useful against the thieving gutter rat. His wrist band unexpectedly rattled against a rock. He froze in place, a heavy boot of a three hundred plus beast pressed his arm into the rock below.

"I didn't expect you to wake so soon. The transporter beacon isn't functioning. We'll have to travel on foot. I'll have to hurry now."

There wasn't a moment of warning or a kind word to prepare him before Stol smashed his boot heel down on his trapped wrist. Aidan cried out and almost lost consciousness. The thin bones shattered in several places, sharp splintered edges grinding into pulverized flesh. He cried out again, vision blurred by agony, as his wrist was forced through the tight bounty band. It landed on the ground by his head, bloodied, the dull glow of its metal, muted in the yellow sand.

The pain was intense but it cleared his mind and focused his resolve. "Why ye doin' this, mate? The challenge's over. There's no profit in this anymore."

"That's where you are wrong, pirate. You are worth a lot of

credits to some people. I'm going to auction you off to the highest bidder. I have debts to pay. Too many debts." Stol forced Aidan to a sitting position, preparing to lift him off the ground. "Humans do not belong on Oracan. Our culture is worth more than a fascinating bed mate."

Aidan Maymon— wait, Aidan of Menalon was tired of being a bloody treasure everyone wanted to steal. His Oracan hunter would be looking for him. Now Aidan needed to slow Stol down long enough for Talos to find him. Or maybe leave a bread crumb behind.

As Stol wrapped Aidan in his arms, the pirate latched on and kissed him full on the mouth. Stol hesitated then returned the kiss, deep and long. The Oracan gasped for air when Aidan could finally break away.

"Talos is well rid of you. He should thank me." Stol swung the pirate over his shoulder like a bag of grain and lumbered off.

Aidan grimaced with the pain and dizziness that accompanied being hung upside down. His broken wrist cradled inadequately with his good arm and hand. The pain threw bright spots of color in his vision, making focusing difficult. Hurriedly, he found the abandoned bounty band in the sand and did something else pirates were very skilled at. He spit. Long and hard, landing a glob of Stol's sour saliva right on the dull surface. He had faith his hunter could smell Stol on the band. Maybe even Doc Jaclyn's magic spells could tell his spit from the Oracans. Either way, he'd left a bread crumb.

Chapter Seventeen

"I think we've got a lead on who poisoned Menalon." Marius had been spending his time investigating the elder Oracan's poisoning along with Zeban while Wacad and Dr. Rice worked on finding a medical way to boost Talos's biological connection with Aidan. He'd felt useless to help his friend out on the medical side. Rooting out a culprit poisoning people was more in his lane of traffic anyway, as the hunter would say. "Your brother arranged a meeting with our suspect. They're in a meeting chamber down the hall. Coming?"

Marius glanced at the two healers behind a glass wall, running tests in a lab unlike any the commander had ever seen before. He was sure Dr. Rice felt like she was in Wonderland. "They know where you'll be. Zeban contacted them. You have time."

Waiting for some sign of progress from the two doctors was driving Talos crazy. He'd tried repeatedly on his own to connect with Aidan, but though there was a connection, he couldn't sense where the pirate was. But at least the runt was alive. "Sure. Why not. Let's fix this part of the puzzle anyway."

It was a short walk from the lab setting to the large meeting chamber in the research center. Guards stood at attention outside the heavy doors, a new addition since earlier. They respectfully parted at the sight of the famed, recently blood-bonded hunter. Talos stiff-armed the doors and the two of them strode in.

Talos's frustrated stride came to a halt at the sight of Chakki seated at table, an apparent serving attendant beside her. Talos didn't recognize the younger one, but Chakki's history with the family firmly supported her not being a suspect.

"What gives?" Talos turned to Marius for an explanation. "Chakki has connived and schemed to be a part of this family since she was waist high. She has been wooing since I got here. How is she a suspect?"

"That's exactly why. This was her bid to do just that." Talos was unconvinced so Marius added, "Poisoning Menalon, or bribing one of your father's staff to do it, got you back home."

"It is true, Talos." Zeban stood off to one side, his diplomatic tone in full use. "You spend so much time away, only returning to accept hunts, she needed a way to draw you here for a long period of time and for less official duties."

"I have done nothing more than my duty to my cashe." Chakki stood and approached Talos, ignoring his partially raised talons on his shoulders and back. Pride and satisfaction radiated off her. "I have long desired to join the two houses of Kaii and Menalon. But nothing seemed to draw you back to Oracan for long, since your brother's death." She held her head high. "But I knew of your deep affection for Menalon. I hoped fanning the flames of family protection and safety would demand that you return for family honor, if nothing else. I was right." She gestured at Talos, proving her point.

"I've told you before, Chakki. I have never had a desire to breed with you. We have no snare between us. That has been proven."

Anger erupted from beneath her cool exterior. "No! *You* have no snare within you. No overwhelming desire to mate, but it is not so for me! I wished to bond with you, but long ago gave up that hope with the failed ritual." She shook with contained rage. "I would be content to merely breed. To join the cashes, produce an heir to your legacy. Our offspring would enjoy great advantages from both family lines." She suddenly turned practical. "The loss of Zeban's mate and your younger brother are both losses for the Menalon linage as well as tragedies." She thrust home her final point. "You will have no heir with your new mate."

Talos stood completely still while thinking about all the points

Chakki had made. Some had merit, but having offspring was not something he desired. That duty was for his older brothers. Zeban could mate again. He'd already had two offspring before his mate had passed. Wacad and Arco were unbonded with plenty of time to do so. The cashe of Menalon would continue without a contribution from him.

"Your desires do not excuse your actions, Chakki."

"I disagree." She assumed her diplomatic air as a Council member. "I plan to summit my actions to the Council for evaluation. No one was permanently harmed. I have no doubt I will be found innocent of any wrong-doing."

"So basically, you poisoned Menalon so you could get your own way?" Marius directed the confession back to the root of the issue. "A bit callous, wouldn't you say?"

"I didn't poison anyone. I merely persuaded Reinda to see the value in assisting me. She coated Menalon's cups with a diluted solution of the poison. Just enough to affect him, not kill him. I like Menalon." Chakki glanced at the silent, frighten serving girl still seated at the table. Reinda stared at the floor, occasionally stealing glances at Zeban and Marius. She was too terrified to even look at Talos. "An heir to the Menalon cashe with the most honored Oracan Hunter is not a minor matter, Commander. It is worth an extra effort."

"Why did Stol declare to challenge for you at the Ritual of Toget?" Talos couldn't figure that one out. "Challenges are dangerous and difficult. No one undertakes them without a stake in the bonding."

"I hired him. If he saw an opportunity to see that your pirate failed the challenge, then so be it." She shrugged, the silky robes draped over her shoulder whispering against her body. "Stol's greed outweighs his sense of personal danger. He accepted that. He is a good merchant. A poor gambler, but a good merchant."

"Where is Stol now?" Talos knew where Jak and Dagi were. Tobi had offered his assistance in finding the kidnapped pirate. Stol had not been seen.

"I have no idea. Our agreement was to be paid only when your pirate failed the ritual. He won. No payment." Chakki shrugged. "I disabled the transporter device I had given to him for the challenge. He can't be far unless he took passage on a ship. His debtors will be unsatisfied." Knowing she had something to hold over Stol's head for all time, Chakki added, "I'd be looking for new way to make credits."

Marius turned away and began speaking rapidly into his communication device, no longer interested in what Chakki had to say.

"I take responsibility for all my actions. I did what any Oracan warrior should do to further her family line and preserve the best of their species. I have acted in accordance with Oracan culture and history." Talos realized Chakki was proud of her actions. Even eager for others to learn of them.

She was establishing herself as a dominant, resourceful female capable of raising a warrior offspring Talos could be proud of. If he was interested. Oracan breeding cycles lasted a very, very long time. The future was always ahead of him. He would concentrate on the one he had with his pirate now.

"The Council will decide your fate, Chakki." Zeban opened the doors to call in the guards. "Until then, you and Reinda will be accompany my security guards."

The two females left, one timid and quiet one leading the way down the hall, guards hurrying to keep her pace. Talos grudgingly admitted to himself Chakki would be a strong mother.

Finishing his conversation, Marius touched Talos's sash. "We have a lead. A residual transporter signature was detected inside of Aidan's room at the treatment center. It was barely there, took several scans to even see the distortion left behind. They pinpointed the last destination out of the room. We have a lock on the location."

§ § § §

The area was bleak. Rough sand and rock in varying shades of orange and yellow, now muted with the falling night's growing shadows that softened the sharp edges and empty horizon. Talos led the rescue party. Marius joined him as had Tobi and Zeban.

It had taken some doing to convince Dr. Rice to stay behind and prepare for Aidan's return. Talos had finally ended the discussion by simply walking out. Moments later, the other males joined him. Wacad had packed everything needed for emergency care and was on-board when they arrived at the craft. The destination was not far from the medical chamber, but it pushed the limits of the distance a small personal transporter might manage with two people in the beam. There was no evidence that a shuttle of any type had landed, the sand undisturbed in the open areas.

Wacad waited by the shuttle, as the others cautiously explored their surroundings, anxious to give the pirate immediate care when he was found.

"He's hurt. I smell Aidan's blood." Nostrils flaring, Talos stalked straight to a section of the ground where the sand was scuffed and the impression of boots distinctly marked the land. He knelt on one knee and dug up a dull metal object hidden by the shifting yellow dust.

"Your band." Zeban scented the air, his hand shifting through the loose sand, pulling up small clumps of blackened dust. "He's bleeding, but not in excessive amounts."

Talos smelled the band, licked it, then crushed it in his fingers. "Stol. I don't know how the runt got him to do it, but Stol left his body fluids behind."

"I don't think I want to know. Let's just be glad he did and go from there." Marius shook his head, scanning their surroundings again and again, making sure no uninvited guests arrived. "Are all Oracan family weddings this...exciting?"

"Your mate is a resourceful creature." Tobi let his admiration show.

"Damn straight he is. Let's see if he can manage to stay alive long enough for us to find him." Talos followed a few tracks but they disappeared as soon as he hit open sand. "The night winds have erased any footprints. There's nothing to track."

"Come back!" Wacad waved a hand in the air. "Dr. Rice requests my help. We need to return."

§ § § §

"Drink." A bitterness was poured in his mouth, making Aidan sputter and choke. It was wet and liquid, but beyond that it was undrinkable, even for a pirate used to bilge water and spoiled meats.

He tried to push away the cup, but his right hand screamed in pain with every twitch of his flesh and his left was too busy trying to hold onto the end of his right arm. It felt as if his hand had been twisted and torn then left dangling. He knew it was swollen to three times its size from the sheer weight of it. His working fingers were covered in dried blood, their grip on his injured wrist forcing them into the mangled flesh just to hold on. Holding on hurt, letting go was worse.

More bitterness slipped down his throat and he tried to jerk his head away but a powerful hand forced him to be still. He swallowed, needing air. The rank fluid burned its way down to his rolling empty stomach, making it queasy all over again.

"I need to get back to my ship, but I need you to be alive when we get there. Drink!" Stol poured more of the Oracan plant juice down Aidan's throat, not minding the way the pirate gagged and resisted. "I need to make sure no one steals you from me. You are all I have standing between the debt collectors and certain death."

There was a certain ring to Stol's voice, a desperation that men backed into a corner find hidden in blackest part of their hearts. A part where compassion and conscience didn't exist. "Never bet more'n ye are willin' ta lose, mate." Aidan wasn't new to gambling. It was a thrilling, if often dangerous, pastime. Stol sounded as if his gambling had gone from fun to desperate madness.

"You are the most valuable prize I've ever gotten my hands on." Stol stared hard at Aidan until the pirate wanted to squirm out of his reach. He could see madness in the violet eyes, read the coldness as it settled into the lines of his gray, pinched face. This was going to hell in a hand basket quickly.

"I can't lose." Stol put down the cup and drew his blade, Aidan threw his body in the opposite direction, but it wasn't enough. He felt the stinging burn as the knife scored his chest, a gaping wound that bleed fiercely. He landed on his back, but the jarring of his injured wrist sent fresh flashes of agony rippling up his body. They exploded at the back of his head. Blackness granted him blissful relief.

§§§§

Wacad and Dr. Rice rushed into the room, injectors clutched in their hands again.

"We have it." Dr. Rice looked at the Oracan healer. "We think we do."

"It's a two-part system." Wacad pressed a thin metal stick against Talos's freshly tattooed arm, centering it on a crimson band. "This is a potentiater, made up of K^8 elements. It will amplify the effects of the booster."

"This is the booster." Dr. Rice slapped her injector into Talos's thick skin, possibly a little more energetically than necessary. "Sorry, this took so much time. I'm not one hundred percent certain it will be the right dosage, but it should work. It has to work. Aidan can't last much longer without medical help."

Talos felt the flow of medication disperse through his body. His bloodstream carried it to every cell, an unusual tingling coursed through his entire body. His mind grew foggy, a slight ache blossomed in the back of his head and the spot where Wacad had placed the K^8 burned like a branding iron. He pushed back at the discomfort, concentrating on the band, on the blood connection, on his pirate.

It took several long moments, but suddenly he heard his mate. The sounds of soft moaning, the gasp of sudden pain, the pounding of his heart, the rhythm regular, but weak and rapid. He felt the extreme pain. Unconsciously, the hunter grasped his own right wrist. He had to focus hard to push the pain away and search for the link, the connection that would tell him more than how Aidan felt. He needed to lock his own internal compass on Aidan's freshly forge blood connection.

Everything depended on his quirky pirate's ability to adapt to his new world, to make the most of his assets, something Aidan had great skill at when his wits were involved. Now it was his biological roadmap's time to work with his adopted Oracan world.

Time dragged on for so long Dr. Rice adjusted her injector and moved to the hunter to deliver another dose. She stopped just short of hitting the injector's activate button when Talos rumbled a hoarse growl. "Got him. They are in the sacred cave in Valley of the Gods. He's dying."

Without a word, Talos grabbed Dr. Rice by her upper arms and vanished.

Chapter Eighteen

Night had fallen. The wind blew more fiercely here, whipping across the wide-open plains, then forcing its way down narrow canyon walls, whispering its singsong chant the Oracan ritual songs were based on. It was the language of the ancient ones, the ones who had prospered and fought and carved out their civilization eons ago. Here in the Valley of the Gods, Oracan hunters learned their fabled tracking skills and warriors honed their brutal fighting ways.

Many a hunt had ended in this sand, the ground steeped in the blood of unlucky bounties sacrificed to the ancient ones. Oracans no longer believed that the gods ruled them, but they still honored the first of their kind in this holy place. Stol had disgraced it with his dishonorable actions. All of Oracan would lay claim to his heart after this. Talos knew it would not still be beating by then.

Talos clamped a hand over the doctor's mouth, using his sash to guard her skin. He didn't need a yapping dame on his hands, he needed silence and stealth until the others joined them. He knew they would be on his heels.

Dr. Rice swallowed her surprise and shut her lips tightly together. She swayed a moment, allowing Talos to steady her, then she pushed his sash off her face. She knew better than to make a noise, but the glare she gave him would blister skin. Human skin, maybe.

Making sure his weapons were securely in place, Talos indicated that Rice stay there, as he crept toward a dull glow at the mouth of sacred cave, the one where the ancients had performed their blood bonding. It was said to possess the spirits of the old ones, granting powers beyond the Ritual of Toget of the present day. It was a law punishable by death to any who entered the cave with the intent to call on the ancient spirits for a blood bond. All Oracans believed in the ancient ones, but Talos left mysticism and the spirit world to others. His world dealt with flesh and blood.

A slight shift in the air pressure told him several others had joined him. He knew Marius, Tobi and Zeban by scent. The others were fellow hunters too numerous to bother sorting out now.

Marius crept up to his side. "Anything?" It was barely a breath of air, but Talos heard him.

Staring into the darkness, he pointed to the left of the cave opening. He touched his heart to indicate that was where Aidan was located. He pointed to the middle of the wide opening and dragged the dull edge of his blade across his throat. Marius got the message. Stol was there. Close to the pirate, but not too near for them to surprise the merchant and safe guard Aidan. Tobi had joined them and nodded then disappeared into the darkness toward the far left of the pale glowing entrance. More hunters fanned out into the night until Talos was left alone with Zeban and Marius.

A burst of pain hit him, both arms burned in unimaginable agony, his whole body flashed white hot. An odd sensation gathered in the pit of one of his stomachs and the world spun. Talos grabbed the flood of agony and hung on to it. He gathered into one place, pulling the threads of pain toward him until they were all in a tight, blazing ball. Then he soothed the round surface, calming it, drawing away the fire until it merely throbbed, a dull shadow of its original pain.

Slightly unsteady, Talos opened his eyes, immediately adjusting to the darkness. His lover was exhausted to almost beyond his limits of endurance. There was no waiting for a better time. Without a word he began creeping toward the cave, his blade prominent in his fist, a sense of urgency in his movements.

"Avast, you slimy, bilge rat! Leave off!" It was part shout of alarm, part cry of agony. Aidan voice was harsh and raspy, but it carried weakly in the still air and ended with a choked moan.

Talos rose up out of the darkness, his full hunter stature amplified by the soft beacon light in the cave, his silhouette against the shinning half-moon creating a dramatic image that spoke to Stol's unraveling mind.

In the midst of forcing more blood from the knife wound on the pirate's chest, the Oracan merchant dropped the cup from his hand. The contents splashed across the ancient rock floor, seeping into the cracks and porous surface.

Aidan moaned and tried unsuccessfully to raise his head when Stol let him drop to the floor.

"No! I need his blood." Stol scrambled to swipe up the disappearing liquid, his hands raking over the empty surface. "No, you don't understand, he has to be mine. The sale of this human will save my business! My reputation!" Stol rose up and faced Talos, his gaze darting back and forth behind the hunter, counting stoic expressions and deadly glares aimed at him.

"Your reputation no longer matters, Stol." Talos moved forward a few precious feet.

"Of course, it does. It's all that matters in business." Stol blustered and puffed his chest out, then shook his head, confused and disoriented suddenly cringing when he got another look at the group of united hunters. It gave Talos pause to see a fellow Oracan shrink before his eyes. The madness was clear. It almost made Talos consider sparing him. Almost.

"Not for you. Because you're history, mack. A goner." Talos stepped closer but Stol suddenly sprung to life, going in the direction Talos feared the most.

"Not alone!" Stol swung around and lifted his leg, aiming the heel of his boot at Aidan's head. He choked at the sound of blade thrusting into flesh, and turned to face the hunter.

Talos grabbed the hilt of his thrown blade buried in the merchant's side and the front of Stol's robes, heaving him bodily out the opening of the cave to the waiting circle of fellow hunters and Zeban. The following sounds were fierce, the tearing of flesh and the breaking of bones, all while deep, guttural voices trilled and chirped in a singsong harmony.

Marius appeared at the cave entrance, shielding Dr. Rice from the worst of the ritual kill a few feet away outside.

"How is he?" Dr. Rice rushed forward to kneel beside Aidan, checking his pulse, applying sealant over the knife wound to stop the bleeding until it could be cleaned and mended. "He needs to transported out of here the second I immobilize this wrist." She strapped small devices to his barely moving chest and injected medication after medication into his arms. "I've given him neuroblockers for the pain. I don't need medical scans to see this wrist is shattered. He's probably got extensive nerve and blood vessel damage, too." She lifted the grossly mangled arm out of the limp grip of his other hand and gently formed an instant split around it. "That's why all the swelling. He must have been in excruciating pain."

"'Twas, me pretty, 'twas." Aidan peeled open one eye and gave the doctor a randy smile. "Been lookin' forward ta seein' ye, Dr. Jaclyn. Got a sword bite needs lookin' after." He tried to lift his right arm off his chest, but neither of them seemed to want to do his bidding.

"Hang in there, runt. We're going home." Talos lifted his pirate off the ground, cradling him in his arms, as Dr. Rice fussed over arranging his broken limb just so.

"Knew ye 'twas here, luv." Aidan opened both eyes and stared solemnly at his lover. "Heard ye in me head again." He closed his eyes and put a pout on his dirty face and then snuggled closer to his mate. "Not sure ye should be doing that much. Gives me head pains."

"I'll give you a pain, runt. Lie still."

A rock slipped under Talos's weight, throwing him slightly off-balance. His freshly tattooed shoulder scraped across the cave wall leaving a smear of his blood behind. It soaked into the thirsty surface, leaving nothing behind.

Suddenly the ground shook. Rocks rolled pasted their feet and crimson dust drifted down from the ceiling, layering all four of them. Choking, Talos rushed out of the cave with Aidan, protecting him with his hunched body as much as he could. Marius did the same for the doctor, guiding her past the others.

None paused to even brush the cave dust from their clothes or skin. By the time they stopped to transport back, the dust had disappeared, swirling away on the night winds.

§ § § §

"Surgery went well. He's in good shape considering all that's happened to him lately." Dr. Rice sighed and leaned against the treatment room wall. "The diagnosis Wacad and I worked out was correct. The K^8 was causing tiny pockets of toxic pus to invade his liver cells, rupturing with stress, mental or physical."

"That wasn't so bad on P6, his life is pretty carefree there, but here? No wonder he got worse once they arrived." Marius watched the bedside monitors flash and pulse, relieved at how regular everything appeared to his non-medical eye. The pirate looked small and very young. "How is he?"

"Well, I had to splint his wrist in the old-fashioned, heat foam cast. I've aligned the splintered bones, of which there were a lot, but until I can adjust the scanners to regenerate his bone and tissues it will have to do. Our scanner isn't able to do it because of the Oracan DNA interference and Oracan's don't come close to helping from a human cellular level. Aidan is somewhere in between." She leaned over and smoothed a wild strand of hair off Aidan's smooth forehead. He was deep in a medically induced sleep post-surgery. "If the Council hadn't agreed to allow sharing of some biodata, we would never have figured out the poison from the band."

"Are you sure? You've done some amazing things in your field, Jaclyn."

"Positive. We didn't even know about K^8. Medical systems don't look for something they don't know exists. It's a huge break-through. Their research facility is to die for." She grinned when Marius rolled his eyes. "Seriously. Wacad's argument to the Council about having an informed physician for medical issues outside of Oracan is even more important now. Both hunter and pirate will need a hybrid medical profile worked up." Her face dropped. "I'll have to re-calibrate every system we have. We'll need two of everything. Oh my gods, my budget!"

§ § § §

"Do ye think she'll ever forgive ye?" Aidan lay sprawled across Talos's naked body, his head positioned so he could trace the swirls and loops on his mate's recently inked chest with his fingertips. It was awkward because his wrist was still in a brace, holding his bones together until Dr. Jaclyn learned how to mend them faster.

"Probably not anytime soon. The dame holds a grudge pretty good." Talos swept one hand over his pirate's smooth back. They had just showered and both were relaxed, sated, for now, and pleasantly warm. They were happy to be in their own bed.

"Odd it was her first inking, don't ye think? Ay'da thought a lady of her high-breedin' would 'ave a few by now."

"Humans don't do that much anymore." Talos huffed and complained, "Don't know why it's all my fault."

"Could be 'cause the Council nicked ye for doin' ye Ceme voodoo and disappearin' in front of her and his High an' Mightiness." Aidan squirmed and let his legs fall to either side of the hunter's broad body, his thighs gently hugging the Oracan's trim waist. He was very comfortable. The fever was gone and his sexual urges were once more his own. The frequency of them hadn't altered much, but the dire urgency had faded to tolerable levels.

"Yeah, well, I had my reasons."

When all the chaos had died away after Aidan's rescue, the Council had seen fit to review Talos and Aidan's time on Oracan. Talos had been praised for his completed mate bond, cautioned about his new mate's proclivity for unorthodox problem-solving, and sanctioned for his violating the time-travel laws. He was not rebuked for using it to rescue Aidan. As a citizen of Oracan, it was done for Aidan's sake, not Talos's. It was a stretch, but Talos had accepted the ruling without comment as did the rest of the Council.

But the Council had not been so forgiving of him teleporting without the camouflage of using a device or ship. No others outside of Oracan knew that Oracan's themselves were the teleporters. He had revealed this to offworlders in front of witnesses.

After much debate, Zeban, supported by Wacad and the Medical Council, persuaded the High Principles that both Marius and Dr. Rice were privy to many Oracan secrets by way of the fact Talos and Aidan lived among them as friends and allies. Additionally, Dr. Rice was now granted access to limited amounts of Oracan medical data. She and the Commander were professionals and could be trusted. In the end, the Council had agreed. Provided both submitted to allowing a small tattoo to be placed on the inner aspect of their right elbow, discrete, but easily spotted by any Oracan in need.

"She liked all the doctor stuff Wacad showed her. 'Twas more 'an happy to get her fingers on those fancy baubles and bits." Talos slipped his hands down Aidan's back to knead his ass cheeks, teasing the sensitive skin between his fleshy globes. He widened legs, moving his knees forward to open his ass to the attention. "Littl' ink's a small price ta pay."

"Even Marius was irritated. And he's sporting markings already. Wuss." Talos hitched his lover's light frame up further on his chest. "But he got over it. Soon as they made him an official ambassador to Oracan. Guess it got him points with the Corporation."

"Should be thankin' us." Turning his head to watch his hunter's expression, Aidan slowly licked over the sensitive breast-plates beneath his face. He thought he'd get more of a response until a slippery eel slithered into his tight ass, poking and twisting its way inside. He moaned and panted. "'Twas like our weddin' gift to them. Ungrateful gobs."

Aidan grinned and clenched his ass, gasping when the eel grew in size, hardening into a firm Oracan cock. Talos moved a hand to pluck at Aidan's hard nipples, twisting and rolling them until they tingled with heat.

He dropped down onto the hunter's chest, lips inches away from his lover's mouth and murmured, "Speakin' of weddin's luv, don't ye owe me a proper weddin' night?"

Talos's only answer was a hoarse, "Ta-ti."

The End

About the Author

Laura Baumbach is the award-winning author of numerous short stories, novellas, novels and screenplays. Her favorite genre to work in is manlove or m/m erotic romances. Manlove is not traditional gay fiction, but erotic romances written specifically for the romantic-minded reader, male or female. Married to the same man for almost 30 years, she currently lives with her husband and two sons in the blustery Northeast of the United States but is looking for a warmer location to spend the second half of her professional and family life.

Laura is the owner of ManLoveRomance Press, founded in January of 2007. You can find Laura on the internet at:

http://www.laurabaumbach.com/

http://groups.yahoo.com/group/laurabaumbachfiction

http://www.mlrpress.com/